PORTRAIT OF ALISON

FRANCIS DURBRIDGE

WILLIAMS AND WHITING

Cover design by

Timo Schroeder

9781912582600

Williams & Whiting (Publishers)

15 Chestnut Grove, Hurstpierpoint,

West Sussex, BN6 9SS

Titles by Francis Durbridge published by Williams & Whiting

1   The Scarf – tv serial
2   Paul Temple and the Curzon Case – radio serial
3   La Boutique – radio serial
4   The Broken Horseshoe – tv serial
5   Three Plays for Radio Volume 1
6   Send for Paul Temple – radio serial
7   A Time of Day – tv serial
8   Death Comes to The Hibiscus – stage play
     The Essential Heart – radio play
     (writing as Nicholas Vane)
9   Send for Paul Temple – stage play
10 The Teckman Biography (tv serial)
11 Paul Temple and Steve (radio serial)
12 Twenty Minutes From Rome

Murder At The Weekend – the rediscovered newspaper serials and short stories

Also published by Williams & Whiting:
Francis Durbridge : The Complete Guide
By Melvyn Barnes

Titles by Francis Durbridge to be published by Williams & Whiting

A Case For Paul Temple
A Game of Murder
A Man Called Harry Brent
A Time of Day
Bat Out of Hell
Breakaway – A Family Affair
Breakaway – The Local Affair
Melissa

This book reproduces Francis Durbridge's original script together with the list of characters and actors of the BBC programme on the dates mentioned, but the eventual broadcast might have edited Durbridge's script in respect of scenes, dialogue and character names.

INTRODUCTION

When Francis Durbridge (1912-98) began writing for BBC television in 1952, he was already the foremost writer of mystery thrillers for BBC radio. In 1938 he had created an enduring formula, when his radio serial *Send for Paul Temple* attracted over 7,000 requests for more. His career on the airwaves blossomed and diversified, mainly under his own name but also occasionally using the pseudonyms Frank Cromwell, Nicholas Vane and Lewis Middleton Harvey. To place him in context, his closest comparators on the radio were Edward J. Mason, Lester Powell, Ernest Dudley, Alan Stranks and Philip Levene.

Send for Paul Temple spawned sequels for thirty years that resulted in an enormous UK and European fanbase, so it was almost inevitable that Durbridge - while continuing to write for radio – turned also to television. Later, in a published interview (*Radio Times*, 21 October 1971) he said: "Twenty years ago in the United States, a producer told me that I was wasting my time by not going into television. So that's what I did – I tried to build up a reputation with serials, since I'd vowed never to write a Paul Temple episode for television."

His television debut was the six-episode serial *The Broken Horseshoe*, transmitted live by the BBC from 15 March to 19 April 1952. This was the first thriller serial on British television, which he quickly followed up with the six-episode serials *Operation Diplomat* (25 October to 29 November 1952) and *The Teckman Biography* (26 December 1953 to 30 January 1954). Then his fourth, *Portrait of Alison*, again consisted of six episodes (16 February to 23 March 1955).

Francis Durbridge's television career was impressive and lasted for almost thirty years, but its success must be credited not only to the writer himself but also to his producer/director

Alan Bromly. From *Portrait of Alison* onwards, the Durbridge/Bromly partnership created a long run of serials that teased viewers with red herrings, cliff-hanger endings to each episode, and the certainty that no character should be believed whatever they might say. And as a result Durbridge's contribution to television drama became iconic, resulting in the recognition that for all his serials from 1960 (beginning with *The World of Tim Frazer*) the BBC awarded him the unprecedented accolade of the "Francis Durbridge Presents" screen credit before the title sequence of each episode.

In *Portrait of Alison* the leading man was the distinguished radio and television actor Patrick Barr (1908-85), who had already been named Outstanding Actor in the *Daily Mail* National Television Awards 1954-55 with a citation that included his role in Durbridge's previous serial *The Teckman Biography*. But it is impossible to resist mentioning the wonderful Brian Wilde (1927-2008), who played David Forester in *Portrait of Alison* and went on to become a Durbridge regular in *The World of Tim Frazer* (1960), *Melissa* (1964) and *A Man Called Harry Brent* (1965) before his long comedy runs as Prison Officer Barrowclough in *Porridge* and Foggy Dewhurst in *Last of the Summer Wine*. And also interesting and unusual is the fact that the actor William Lucas (1925-2016) played the blackmailing car dealer Reg Dorking in both the television serial and the subsequent film.

Turning to the cinema, it is not surprising that *Portrait of Alison* quickly became a film because movie versions of Durbridge's early Paul Temple radio serials and his first three television serials had proved popular. *Portrait of Alison* (Insignia/Anglo Amalgamated, 1955) did not use Durbridge as screenwriter, but instead the screenplay was by Ken Hughes and Guy Green and the Director was Guy Green. While it is clear from Durbridge's recently discovered script that his television serial was in many ways better than the film, this might be a little unfair as a television serial lasting three hours must inevitably require editing when adapted as an eighty-four minute movie. In spite of this, however, film makers always seemed able to add action scenes and fights in order to please cinemagoers!

In this case Major Colby is excluded from the film, with the television Inspector Layton becoming the combined Inspector Colby. David Forester, a schoolmaster with a substantial role in the serial, is reduced to an action-man figure in the film; Henry Carmichael is a much smaller role in the film, as is Peter Fenby; and Alison's father Norman Briggs becomes John Smith with a reduced role, while Mary Hepburn does not appear in the film at all. Overall, therefore, we can see that the television serial presented a more comprehensive mix of Durbridge's traditional twists, turns and cliff-hangers.

The film's co-stars Robert Beatty and Terry Moore, both cinema favourites in the 1950s, replaced Patrick Barr and Helen Shingler – which was common practice, as film producers usually opted for proven movie stars rather than television actors. Indeed Patrick Barr had already experienced this when, irrespective of his achievement in the *Daily Mail* National Television Awards, he was replaced for the film *The Teckman Mystery* by John Justin.

As usual there was interest abroad – with the film released in the USA as *Postmark for Danger*, in Italy as *Il segno del pericolo*, in Denmark as *Farlig post*, in Finland as *Kuolema saapuu postitse* and in Brazil as *Carta a um Assassinato*. A DVD of the original British film was released much later, by Studiocanal/Network in 2014.

Portrait of Alison was later novelised (Hodder & Stoughton, August 1962), and a US edition was published slightly earlier (Dodd, Mead, March 1962). But inevitably there have been foreign translations – in Germany as *Das Kennwort*, in France as *Le Portrait d'Alison*, in Italy as *Ritratto di Alison*, in The Netherlands as *Portret van Alison* and also as *De zaak Alison*, in Poland as *Portret Alison* and in Croatia as *Alisonin Portret*.

So we have the film and we have the novel, but now for the first time we have Durbridge's original television script. Certainly one to enjoy!

Melvyn Barnes
Author of Francis Durbridge: The Complete Guide (Williams & Whiting, 2018)

PORTRAIT OF ALISON

A serial in six episodes

By FRANCIS DURBRIDGE

Broadcast on BBC TV

Feb 16th – Mar 23rd 1955

CAST:

Tim Forester	Patrick Barr
Jill Stewart	Elaine Dundy
David Forester	Brian Wilde
Det. Insp. Layton	Lockwood West
Major Colby	Anthony Nicholls
Norman Briggs	Arnold Bell
Henry Carmichael	Peter Dyneley
Reg Dorking	William Lucas
Alison Ford	Helen Shingler
Mary Hepburn	Elaine Wodson
Peter Fenby	William Kendall
Det. Sgt. Reed	Edward Dain
Nurse	Anne Ridler
Charles White	Patrick Jordan
Hospital Sister	Grace Webb
Chambermaid	Gretchen Franklin

EPISODE ONE

OPEN TO: The Studio Flat of TIM FORESTER, a successful portrait painter. The studio is the top floor of a house in Eaton Square, London. It is spacious and well furnished. The room is used as a living room as well as a studio. There are an occasional table with telephone, settee, wingchair, drinks cabinet etc. There is a raised dais at the end of the room. The front door of the studio is through an alcove. Other doors lead to the bedrooms, bathroom, kitchen etc.

TIM FORESTER, a good-looking man in his early thirties, is painting JILL STEWART. JILL is a professional model; pert, young, attractive. She is sitting on a chair on the dais facing TIM. There is nothing chi-chi or arty-crafty about either TIM or the studio. Music is coming from a small radio on a side table.

JILL: Nearly finished?

TIM: Yes. Tired?

JILL: M'm – a little bit. (*A moment*) How's the housekeeper situation?

TIM: (*Not looking up; a shrug*) About the same …

JILL: Why don't you advertise for one?

TIM: (*After a moment; studying the canvas*) M'm?

JILL: I said – why don't you advertise for one?

There is a pause. TIM looks at the canvas; then he puts down his brush and palette, turns away from the easel, and switches off the radio. JILL rises and crosses down to TIM.

TIM: I take it you don't read The Times, Miss Stewart?

JILL: No, I'm afraid I don't.

TIM: You should. My advertisements are a regular feature. I feel more like a contributor than an advertiser.

JILL: (*Laughing*) For two pins I'd take the job on myself.

TIM: For two pins I'd let you.

3

JILL: (*Smiling*) Well – why not?

TIM: (*Very serious*) Can you make coffee: good, strong, black coffee.

JILL: I'm much better on martinis.

TIM: (*Laughing*) Yes, I'll bet you are!

JILL picks up her fur stole and sits on the arm of a chair; she is facing TIM.

JILL: You know, it's an extraordinary thing. I've been coming here every day for almost two weeks, sitting in that chair, watching you paint, and yet I don't know a thing about you. Except that you're a bachelor, you haven't a housekeeper, and you like strong black coffee.

TIM: Well – what would you like to know?

JILL: What sort of a person are you? What sort of books do you read? Why haven't you taken me out to dinner?

TIM: (*Smiling*) Shall we take the forty-dollar question first? I haven't invited you out to dinner because of something your agent said the first day he brought you here.

JILL: My agent?

TIM: Yes. He said you were an extremely good model but inclined to be possessive.

JILL: Well, really!

TIM: He also said if I got too friendly you'd tell me the story of your life. I gather it's a short life but a very, very long story.

JILL: Is there anything else I ought to know about myself?

TIM: (*Quietly*) Yes. He said you were engaged to an extremely nice man, called Henry Carmichael.

JILL: (*A shade annoyed*) He'd no right to tell you that.

TIM: Why not? Isn't it true?

4

JILL: Yes – but that's not the point.

TIM: I think it is the point. Would your fiancé like it if I took you out to dinner?

JILL: Oh, don't be silly! He wouldn't know a thing about it.

TIM: Wouldn't he! We'd probably find him sitting at the very next table.

JILL laughs, then crosses to the table and casually – almost without thinking – picks up a postcard which is on the table.

TIM: Can you make ten o'clock tomorrow morning, Miss Stewart, instead of eleven.

JILL: Look, even if you don't want to take me out to dinner, don't you think we ought to drop this Mr Forester – Miss Stewart nonsense?

TIM: (*Smiling*) Yes, of course.

JILL: Yes, of course, Jill!

TIM: Yes, of course, Jill.

JILL: Ten o'clock?

TIM: (*Nodding*) That's fine.

JILL looks at the postcard she is holding and is obviously amused. The postcard bears a Naples postmark and shows a rough and rugged exaggerated sketch of a young man sitting under a palm tree; there is an ice bucket with champagne in it by his side. A hand-written message reads: "Still keeping my nose to the grindstone. Regards, Lewis."

JILL: Who's Lewis.

TIM: He's my brother.

JILL: He seems to have the right idea! Where is he in the South of France?

TIM: No, I think he's in Italy at the moment. He dashes all over the place. He's foreign correspondent to the London Gazette.

JILL: Why, yes, of course! Forester … Lewis Forester!

TIM: That's right. Have you met him?

5

JILL: Yes, once – a long time ago? He wrote a book called 'Europe Inside Out'.

TIM: Yes, that's right.

JILL: It was fascinating.

TIM: (*Surprised*) Did you read it?

JILL: Yes. (*Amused*) I can read, you know – didn't my agent tell you? Have you any other brothers?

TIM: One – David. He's the really clever one. Winchester; Jesus College, Cambridge, the whole bag of tricks.

JILL: And what does he do for a living?

TIM: He's a housemaster at a public school just outside St. Albans. Now supposing you tell me about Henry?

JILL: There's not a great deal to tell. We met at a house party about six months ago. He proposed and I accepted. He's a farmer.

TIM: (*Surprised*) A farmer!

JILL: Yes, and I know exactly what you're thinking! You can't imagine me as a farmer's wife.

TIM: Well, it rather depends on the farmer!

JILL: Oh, Henry's a professional all right. He's got the finest herd of – what do you call those things, the black and white ones?

TIM: Cows …

JILL: Yes, I know, but –

TIM: (*Laughing*) Fresians.

JILL: That's it, Fresians. I never can remember that name. He's got the finest herd of Fresians in Berkshire.

TIM: (*Seriously; pulling her leg*) You must be very proud.

JILL: (*Amused, in spite of herself*) Ten o'clock tomorrow morning, Mr Forester.

6

TIM laughs and they cross towards the alcove.

CUT TO: The Entrance Hall of TIM's flat.
TIM is opening the front door for JILL. DAVID FORESTER is in the doorway about to press the bell button. DAVID is tall and rather studious looking; he carries a zip-travelling bag.
TIM: (*Surprised*) Why, hello, David!
DAVID: (*Quietly; very serious*) Hello, Tim!
TIM: This is a surprise! Come in, old boy.
JILL: See you tomorrow.
JILL takes hold of the front door.
TIM: Yes, all right, Jill.

CUT TO: The Living Room / Studio of TIM's flat.
TIM and David enter.
TIM: Why didn't you tell me you were coming into Town? We could have had lunch together.
TIM crosses to the drinks cabinet.
DAVID: (*Softly*) Tim …
TIM: (*Turning; smiling*) Yes?
DAVID: I'm afraid I've got some very bad news.
TIM: (*Puzzled*) What do you mean? (*Alarmed*) David, what's happened?
DAVID: Lewis has had an accident – a car accident, he's … (*He stops*)
TIM: (*Crossing towards DAVID*) You don't mean?
DAVID: (*Nodding*) His car skidded and crashed into a wall. He was killed instantaneously.
TIM: (*Stunned*) Good God! (*Suddenly*) But where? When? How did this happen?
DAVID: I don't know the details; apparently it happened last night, somewhere between Amalfi and Positano.
TIM: But how do you know?

7

DAVID: A man called Fenby telephoned me: he's on the Gazette.

TIM: Yes, I've met him. He was a friend of Lewis's.

DAVID: The paper's chartered a special plane, Fenby's flying out there this afternoon. One of us must go with him, Tim.

TIM: (*Softly; stunned*) Yes, of course.

DAVID: Would you like to go?

TIM: We'll both go, David.

DAVID: No, there's no point in that.

DAVID takes TIM by the arm.

DAVID: Look, leave this to me. I'm very much better at this sort of thing anyway; besides, I speak Italian.

TIM: (*His thoughts elsewhere*) What about your passport – is it all right?

DAVID: Yes.

TIM: (*Suddenly; looking up*) David, you don't think there's any mistake about this? I mean, sometimes … news from abroad …

DAVID: (*Shaking his head*) No. No, there's no mistake.

TIM lights a cigarette: he stands staring down at the postcard which JILL has replaced on the table.

TIM: Lewis … My God, I can hardly believe it. Why, I had a postcard from him only yesterday …

DAVID: (*After a moment*) Tim, I think I'd like a drink. Have you got any scotch?

TIM: Yes, of course.

TIM returns to the drinks cupboard: he takes out glasses and a Whisky decanter. DAVID crosses and picks up the postcard; he stands looking at it for a moment and then puts it down.

TIM: Was there anyone else with him?

DAVID: (*Puzzled*) What do you mean?

TIM: In the car?

8

DAVID: I don't know. I'm afraid I didn't ask. (*Thoughtfully*) I never thought of that.

The telephone starts to ring.

DAVID: That's probably Fenby. I told him he could reach me here.

DAVID crosses and picks up the receiver. TIM watches him.

DAVID: (*On the phone*) Hello? … Yes, this is David Forester … Hello, Fenby … No, he's not, I'm coming … Where? … What time? … Three o'clock … Yes, all right. I'll see you at the Airport. (*Suddenly*) Oh, Fenby – was there anyone else in the car? (*Surprised*) A girl? … Who was she, do you know? (*A long pause*) I see. All right, I'll see you at three o'clock.

DAVID puts down the receiver.

DAVID: There was a girl with Lewis – an actress, apparently she was a friend of his. Her name was Alison Ford.

TIM: I've never heard of her. Was she killed?

DAVID nods.

CUT TO: Living Room / Studio of TIM's Flat.

JILL is sitting on the chair on the dais. TIM is working on the portrait; the portrait is now finished, he is merely adding one or two quite unnecessary touches.

JILL: Is it finished?

TIM: (*A sigh*) I suppose so.

JILL: You don't seem very certain.

TIM: I'd like to scrap it and start the whole thing all over again.

JILL rises and comes down to the easel.

JILL: Yes, well, not this morning, thank you very much.

JILL glances at her wristlet watch.

9

JILL:	My goodness, I must fly! I've got a fitting at twelve o'clock.
TIM:	(*Smiling at JILL*) Thank you, Jill. You've been very patient, especially during the past week.
JILL:	(*Touching TIM's arm; a simple gesture*) Yes, it hasn't been easy for you, has it? I hope I shall see you again, Tim.
TIM:	I hope so too. Perhaps you'd like to have dinner with me one evening …
JILL:	(*Delighted*) Why, I'd love to!
TIM:	… with Henry, of course.
JILL:	(*Disappointed*) Of course! (*Suddenly, with a laugh*) Well, if you ever find yourself marooned in Upper Netherington, give me a ring.
TIM:	(*Surprised*) Upper Netherington?
JILL:	Yes.
TIM:	Do you mean Upper Netherington in Berkshire?
JILL:	That's right.
TIM:	Is that where you're going to live when …
JILL:	(*Nodding*) Mrs Henry Carmichael, Foxdown Farm, Upper Netherington, Berks.
TIM:	But that's extraordinary!
JILL:	I couldn't agree with you more!
TIM:	No, no, you don't understand. I've got a cottage at Melford – a weekend cottage – it's about three miles from Upper Netherington.
JILL:	Really? Why, that's wonderful! We'll be practically neighbours.
TIM:	Just a minute! Henry Carmichael … Foxdown Farm … The penny's beginning to drop … He's fabulously wealthy!

JILL takes out her powder compact and lipstick.

JILL:	Of course he is, Sweetie – you don't think I'd put up with all those black and white things if he

	wasn't fabulously wealthy. I'm hoping he'll start a small holding in Regents Park.
TI M:	(*Laughing*) Jill, you're incorrigible!
JILL:	When are you going down to Melford again?
TIM:	Probably at the weekend, I'm not sure yet.

The front doorbell rings.

JILL:	Well, give me a ring, we're having a cocktail party. Netherington 17.
TIM:	Cocktail parties aren't much in my line, you ought to know that by now.
JILL:	(*Making up her face*) They're not in Henry's, but he's having one. The poor darling's forty on Saturday. He'll need something to cheer him up.

TIM smiles and goes out through the alcove.

CUT TO: The Entrance Hall of TIM's flat.

TIM is opening the front door. DETECTIVE INSPECTOR LAYTON and MAJOR COLBY are standing in the doorway. LAYTON is a well-dressed, pleasant looking man about fifty-two or three: he does not wear a mackintosh. COLBY is in his forties, he has a casual, rather disarming manner.

LAYTON: Mr Forester?

TIM: Yes.

LAYTON: My name is Layton, sir – Detective-Inspector Layton. This is a colleague of mine, Major Colby.

TIM: (*Surprised*) Er, good morning …

LAYTON: (*Smiling*) Could you spare us a moment, sir – we'd rather like to have a word with you?

TIM: Why, yes. Yes, of course. Come in!

LAYTON: Thank you, sir.

CUT TO: Living Room / Studio of TIM's Flat.

JILL has finished making her face up and is replacing her compact. She turns towards the alcove as TIM re-enters with the INSPECTOR and COLBY.

TIM: (*Rather lost for words; to COLBY and LAYTON*)
            This is a … friend of mine.

JILL gives TIM 'a look'.

LAYTON: (*Politely*) How do you do?

COLBY smiles at JILL and gives a little nod.

TIM: Detective-Inspector Layton and Major … er –?

COLBY: Colby.

TIM: Major Colby.

JILL: (*Smiling*) Hello!

There is a pause. JILL looks at the INSPECTOR, then at COLBY, and finally at TIM.

JILL: Well, I'll be making a move.

TIM: Yes, all right, Jill.

JILL: Hope to see you at the weekend, if not before.

JILL stops TIM as he moves towards the alcove.

JILL: No, it's all right, I can let myself out.

JILL crosses, stops by TIM, looks at the INSPECTOR and COLBY, and then to TIM's astonishment, kisses him.

JILL: Goodbye, darling.

JILL goes out. TIM looks at COLBY and the INSPECTOR, he is faintly embarrassed.

TIM: Miss Stewart works for me.

LAYTON: I see, sir.

TIM: She's a sort of – sort of model.

LAYTON: (*Politely*) A sort of model, sir.

TIM: (*A shade aggressive*) Well, I mean she is a model;
            a very good one.

LAYTON: Yes, I'm sure, sir. Well, we can see you're a very
            busy man, Mr Forester, so we'll come straight to
            the point.

LAYTON looks at COLBY.

COLBY: Just over a week ago, your brother – Mr Lewis Forester – was killed in a motor car accident.

TIM: Yes.

COLBY: We're making certain routine inquiries about the accident and we thought perhaps you might be able to help us.

TIM: Why, yes, by all means – if I can. Please sit down …

COLBY: Thank you.

COLBY sits in the wing chair. The INSPECTOR remains standing.

TIM: (*Indicating a chair*) Inspector?

LAYTON: I'm all right, sir – thank you.

COLBY: (*Pleasantly*) When did you last hear from your brother, Mr Forester?

TIM: I had a postcard from him the day before he was killed.

COLBY: Indeed? Have you got the card, sir?

TIM: Yes, I have.

COLBY: I'd like to see it if you don't mind.

TIM crosses, opens a drawer in a side table, and returns to COLBY with the postcard.

COLBY: (*Taking the card*) Thank you, sir.

COLBY examines the card.

COLBY: (*Smiling*) Your brother seems to have been rather fond of these little drawings.

TIM: Yes, they were typical of Lewis. Actually, some of them were not too bad.

COLBY: (*Returning the card to TIM*) Have you got any other postcards like this, sir?

TIM: Yes, I believe I've got one other …

COLBY: (*With charm*) Could I see it?

TIM looks at COLBY, then at the INSPECTOR.

TIM: It's in my bedroom …
COLBY: Thank you, sir.

TIM hesitates a moment, and then goes into the bedroom. COLBY looks at the INSPECTOR, then rises and walks over to the easel. He looks at the painting for a moment, turning as TIM returns from the bedroom. TIM hands COLBY another postcard which COLBY looks at. The card bears an Italian – Sorrento – postmark and shows an exaggerated sketch of a young man swimming in the sea against a background of swaying Palm Trees and a blazing sun. A handwritten message reads: "Don't you wish you were a Foreign Correspondent? Love to David, Lewis." COLBY returns the cards to TIM.

COLBY: Thank you, Mr Forester.

TIM: Now would you mind telling me what this <u>routine</u> inquiry is all about?

COLBY: Just over a fortnight ago your brother sent a postcard to someone; it was posted in Naples and it had a little sketch on it.

COLBY points to the card in TIM's hand.

COLBY: Rather that sort of thing, except that the sketch depicted a hand, I think possibly a girl's hand, holding a bottle of wine. Italian wine, Chianti.

TIM: (*Puzzled*) Well?

COLBY: Did you ever receive a card like that, Mr Forester?

TIM: No.

COLBY: You're sure?

TIM: Yes, I'm quite sure. Was there a message on the card?

LAYTON: (*Hesitating*) We don't think so, sir.

TIM: But look here, Lewis wouldn't send anyone a card with just a drawing on it. It doesn't make sense. He only did the drawings as a sort of, well – leg-pull, to illustrate a private joke, as it were.

14

LAYTON: (*Quietly*) I think this particular card was rather an exception, sir.

TIM: (*Puzzled*) Have you spoken to anyone else about this?

COLBY: Such as?

TIM: Well, my brother – David – for instance?

LAYTON: (*Nodding*) Yes, we saw Mr Forester this morning. We came straight here from St Albans.

TIM: Well, what did David have to say about it?

LAYTON: He couldn't help us.

TIM: This card – is it just an ordinary postcard that Lewis sent to someone, a friend of his, perhaps?

LAYTON: (*After a glance at COLBY*) Yes.

COLBY: Unfortunately, we don't know who he sent it to.

TIM: Well, if it's just an ordinary postcard why are you so interested in it?

COLBY: It looks like an ordinary postcard.

TIM: But in actual fact it isn't?

COLBY: (*After a moment*) In actual fact it isn't. (*He holds out his hand*) You've been most co-operative. I'm sorry we had to disturb you.

TIM: Now just a minute! I don't know whether I've been co-operative or not, but you certainly haven't! What's this all about?

COLBY: (*Disarmingly*) But we've told you what it's all about. Your brother sent someone a postcard. It had a particular drawing on it. We'd like to know who he sent it to – and we'd like the card. (*Smiling*) It's as simple as that.

TIM: Yes, but why?

COLBY: (*Blandly*) Why, what?

TIM: (*Emphatically*) Why do you want the card?

COLBY: (*After a moment: quietly*) We'll tell you that when we've found it, Mr Forester.

15

COLBY and the INSPECTOR turn towards the alcove. LAYTON stops and looks at the painting.

LAYTON: Excuse me, sir. Isn't that the young lady you introduced us to?

TIM: Yes.

LAYTON: (*Rather pleased with himself*) I thought I recognised her.

TIM gives the INSPECTOR a look as he and COLBY move towards the alcove.

CUT TO: The front door of TIM FORESTER's studio flat.

A cream, distinguished-looking door, with ornate door knocker, bell push, letter-box and a neat brass plate bearing the name of TIM FORESTER. A man's gloved hand appears and presses the bell push.

NORMAN BRIGGS is the man pushing the bell push. He is in his early fifties; a short, stout, shrewd North countryman. He wears glasses, a loose overcoat and a grey homburg hat. He carries an extremely large folder under his left arm; this contains photographs. After a moment he presses the bell for a second time. The door is opened by TIM.

CUT TO: The Entrance Hall of TIM's flat.

BRIGGS: (*A slight North country accent*) Mr Forester?

TIM: Yes?

BRIGGS: Good afternoon! You don't know me, sir – my name is Briggs. Norman Briggs.

TIM: Well?

BRIGGS: It is Mr Tim Forester, the artist?

TIM: Yes.

BRIGGS: I've called about having a portrait done, Mr Forester.

TIM: A portrait … done …?

BRIGGS: Yes, I want a portrait painting of my daughter. I understand you go in for that sort of thing?

TIM: (*Faintly amused*) Well, yes – I suppose I do.

BRIGGS: Well, do you think we might have a little chat about it?

TIM obviously hesitates.

BRIGGS: If it's awkward this afternoon I'll drop in sometime tomorrow.

TIM: Well – er …

BRIGGS: Perhaps I should have telephoned for an appointment?

TIM: (*Suddenly making up his mind; rather amused still*) No, no, that's all right, Mr Briggs. Please come in!

BRIGGS: Thank you.

BRIGGS enters the hall.

CUT TO: Living Room / Studio of TIM's Flat.

Tim enters followed by BRIGGS.

TIM: Shall I take your coat?

BRIGGS: (*Looking round the studio*) Oh, thank you.

BRIGGS takes off his coat and hands it, with his hat, to TIM. TIM takes them into the hall. He then re-enters.

BRIGGS: (*Still staring round at the various pictures, easel, etc*) Well, it all looks very interesting and very industrious. (*He smiles at TIM*) This is the first time I've been in an artist's studio.

TIM: I see.

TIM points to the wing chair.

BRIGGS: (*Sitting down*) Thank you.

BRIGGS puts the folder down by the side of the chair.

TIM: I take it I was recommended to you by someone?

BRIGGS: (*Shaking his head*) No. Your brother's word was good enough for me, Mr Forester.

TIM: (*Surprised*) My brother?

BRIGGS: He said you were the finest portrait painter in London. So when I had this idea, about the picture I mean, I said to myself, well obviously he's the chap.

TIM: (*Smiling*) So my brother recommended me?

BRIGGS: Well, yes, I suppose he did, if you like to put it that way. But it was hardly a recommendation because at that time I'd no idea I'd be going in for this sort of thing.

TIM is obviously faintly puzzled by BRIGGS.

TIM: You're referring to my brother David, I take it?

BRIGGS: David? No, no, Lewis ... Lewis Forester.

TIM: When did you meet Lewis?

BRIGGS: About a month ago, in Milan. I was in Italy on business and we both happened to be staying at the same hotel. About a week later I moved down to Sorrento. I'd only been there a couple of days when Lewis turned up.

TIM: I see. You heard about the accident, of course?

BRIGGS looks at TIM for a moment.

BRIGGS: (*Quietly; with almost a sigh*) Yes, I heard about it. (*Shaking his head*) He was a lovely chap; I don't think I've ever met anyone with quite his – well, I suppose most people would call it charm, but it went deeper than that. There was a quiet, profound sincerity about your brother, Mr Forester. Oh, I know he was an intellectual, but he kept his feet on the ground.

TIM: Yes, we – were very fond of Lewis.

BRIGGS: (*Nodding*) You'd reason to be. You don't meet men like Lewis Forester every day, an' more's the pity. This is the age of the smart alec, the smooth operator, the slick talker. I often used to say to my

18

	daughter, it's not brains you want today, it's a silver tongue, the voice of the nightingale.
TIM:	Did your daughter ever meet him?
BRIGGS:	(*Faintly surprised*) Lewis?
TIM:	Yes.
BRIGGS:	(*Quietly*) She was in the car the night he was killed.
TIM:	(*Rising: staggered*) But surely …
BRIGGS:	(*Nodding*) They were both killed instantaneously. The car skidded and went over a precipice. It was on that dangerous bit of road between Amalfi and Positano.
TIM:	But I thought the girl in the car was called …
BRIGGS:	Alison Ford. Ford was my wife's middle name; when Alison went on the stage, she decided to use it instead of Briggs. I can't say I blame her. Alison Ford. Sounds better than Alison Briggs, doesn't it?
TIM:	Mr Briggs, I'd no idea who you were or I should have …
BRIGGS:	That's all right, don't worry. It's very kind of you to see me at a moment's notice. I appreciate it.
TIM:	(*Puzzled*) You said you wanted me to paint a portrait of your daughter. You don't mean a – portrait of Alison?
BRIGGS:	Yes.
TIM:	But how –?
BRIGGS:	(*Picking up the folder from the side of his chair*) I want you to do it from coloured photographs, Mr Forester. Oh, I know it's a bit unusual, an' it might be a bit tricky, but I want you to try.
TIM:	(*Pointing to the folder*) Are those the photographs?
BRIGGS:	Yes.

TIM: Let me look at them.

BRIGGS opens the folder and takes out three photographs. One is a head and shoulders of ALISON FORD. The other two are identical; full-length photographs of ALISON in a ballet length evening dress. She is an attractive girl in her late twenties. TIM takes the photographs and studies them for a moment; then he puts one on a small easel on the dais. He stands looking at it: after a moment he turns towards BRIGGS who stands watching him.

TIM: (*Pointing*) Can you get me the dress – the one in the photograph?

BRIGGS: Yes, I think so.

TIM: (*After a moment: nodding*) All right, Mr Briggs. Get me the dress and I'll have a shot at it.

BRIGGS: (*Pleased*) Thank you. I was hoping you'd say that.

TIM: (*Turning towards BRIGGS*) You must have met my other brother, David – he flew out to Italy as soon as we heard about Lewis.

BRIGGS: Yes, I know he did; unfortunately, I missed him. You see, I was in Sicily when the accident happened. It took them three days to find me and then I had to get back to Sorrento.

TIM: What a dreadful shock it must have been!

BRIGGS: It was. I just couldn't believe it. As a matter of fact, I didn't believe it, not for twenty-four hours. I thought there'd been some kind of a mix-up.

TIM: Why did your daughter stay behind – in Sorrento, I mean? Was it because …

BRIGGS: Because of Lewis. You see, Alison had met him in Milan and when he turned up in Sorrento … (*A shrug*) There was no keeping them apart.

TIM nods: he looks at the photograph that he has put on the easel.

TIM: (*Quietly*) What a horrible thing to have happened.

BRIGGS: Yes … She was twenty-seven. It's not very old, is it, Mr Forester?

TIM: (*Still looking at the photograph*) It certainly isn't. (*Suddenly; pleasantly*) Mr Briggs, would you like a cup of tea?

BRIGGS: (*Delighted*) Why, that's very nice of you.

TIM: Or perhaps coffee?

BRIGGS: No, no, tea's more in my line – if it's all right by you?

TIM: Yes, that's fine.

TIM goes towards the kitchen.

TIM: I'm afraid I've got to make it myself, I haven't got a housekeeper at the moment.

BRIGGS: Oh, well now, don't put yourself to any trouble, not on my account.

TIM: (*Smiling*) No trouble at all.   I'm very good at making tea.

BRIGGS: (*Laughing*) I'm very good at drinking it.

TIM goes into the kitchen. BRIGGS turns and looks round the studio; then he looks towards the kitchen. It is difficult to tell what he is thinking. After a moment he takes out a cigarette case and a lighter. He puts a cigarette in his mouth and flicks the lighter.

CUT TO: Eaton Square, London. Late afternoon: two days later.

A taxi drives up to one of the large houses in the Square. JILL STEWART gets out of the taxi; she is laden with parcels. She pays the taxi driver, then crosses towards the house.

CUT TO: Living Room / Studio of TIM's Flat.

TIM is working on the portrait of ALISON FORD. He is sketching a brief outline of the proposed portrait. The three photographs of ALISON are on view, propped on chairs or easels etc. There is a headless dummy 'model' on the dais; the model is wearing the dress worn by ALISON in the photographs. TIM stops drawing and stares at the dress; after a moment he crosses to the model and makes one or two alterations to the folds of the dress. Tim returns to the easel but as he gets there the doorbell rings.

CUT TO: The Entrance Hall of TIM's flat.
TIM enters from the living room / studio and opens the front door. JILL is standing in the doorway; she has been shopping and carries several parcels.

TIM: (*Surprised*) Why, hello, Jill!

JILL: Hi!

TIM: (*Pointing to the parcels*) What have you been up to?

JILL: I've been shopping …

TIM: (*Laughing*) No …

JILL: Well, aren't you going to ask me in?

TIM: (*After a momentary hesitation*) Yes, of course.

JILL enters and TIM closes the front door.

TIM: Is there anything left in Bond Street?

JILL: A few odds and ends.

CUT TO: The living room / studio of TIM's flat.
JILL enters followed by TIM.

JILL: I gather you haven't got a housekeeper yet?

TIM: No. (*A shade briskly*) Well – what can I do for you, Jill?

JILL: (*Looking round the studio*) My word, you do sound businesslike.

TIM: I don't want to be rude but I've an awful lot to do and I'm due at St Albans at seven o'clock.

JILL: St Albans?

TIM: Yes. I'm dining with my brother.

22

JILL: Oh, yes, of course! He's got a school or something, hasn't he?
TIM: He's a Housemaster.
JILL: At a boys' school?
TIM: Well, he wouldn't be a Housemaster at a girls' school, would he?
JILL: He would if he were smart.

JILL puts her parcels down on the table, turns and looks round the studio. She is intrigued by the photographs of ALISON and the dress.

JILL: Hello! What's all this in aid of?
TIM: I'm painting a portrait of a girl called Alison Ford.
JILL: From photographs?
TIM: Yes.
JILL: If she wants her portrait painting why doesn't she come and sit for you?
TIM: She was killed in a motorcar accident; I'm painting the portrait for her father.
JILL: Oh, I see.

JILL crosses and looks at one of the photographs.

JILL: She's rather good-looking.
TIM: Yes; she was a friend of Lewis's – my brother …

JILL crosses and steps onto the dais; she walks round the model, examining the dress.

JILL: (*Intrigued*) This is the dress in the photograph, isn't it?
TIM: Yes.
JILL: That's an awfully good idea; having the actual dress, I mean.
TIM: Don't touch it, Jill!
JILL: (*Moving round the model; peering at the dress*) It's very sweet …
TIM: Jill, please don't touch it.

JILL puts her hands behind her back and walks round the model, then she comes down from the dais and joins TIM.

JILL: Isn't it going to be awfully difficult for you, painting from photographs?

TIM: It's not going to be easy; it needs a lot of concentration.

JILL: That sounds remarkably like a hint!

TIM: Jill, I'm delighted to see you, really delighted, but–

JILL: (*Laughing*) Scram!

JILL picks up a large parcel off the table.

JILL: I wonder if you'd do something for me?

TIM: What is it?

JILL: You said you were probably going down to Melford at the weekend.

TIM: Yes, I am.

JILL: Well, it's Henry's birthday on Saturday and …

TIM: Yes, you told me, he's forty …

JILL: … I shan't be able to see him.

TIM: But I thought you mentioned a cocktail party?

JILL: Yes, I know. It's infuriating; I've got to work all day Saturday and probably the best part of Sunday too.

TIM: I say, that is bad luck.

JILL: I'm furious about the whole thing, but there's nothing I can do. It's entirely my agent's fault. He's cooked up some cock-eyed publicity stunt or other.

TIM: Well, what do you want me to do, Jill?

JILL: (*Handing TIM the parcel*) Henry's birthday present, I'd like you to deliver it to him …

TIM: Can't you post it?

JILL: Darling, it's breakable and I don't want to take the risk – besides it won't take you five minutes to run over to Henry's place.

TIM: Yes, all right.

JILL: I telephoned him this morning. He's expecting you. Foxdown Farm, Upper Netherington …

TIM: Yes, I know. All right Jill.

TIM puts the parcel down near the chair on the dais.

JILL: Now don't forget it!

TIM: I shan't.

JILL moves towards the dais and looks at the dress again.

JILL: That is a pretty dress!

TIM glances at his watch, then picks up the rest of the parcels off the table and piles them onto JILL.

TIM: Jill, please don't think I'm rude …

JILL: Give Henry my love …

TIM gently leads JILL towards the alcove.

TIM: Yes, of course I will.

JILL: (*Suddenly stopping TIM*) And Tim, there's just one point – do be careful what you say.

TIM: What do you mean – be careful what I say?

JILL: I mean, about us. Don't let him think we're terribly friendly.

TIM: But we're not terribly friendly!

JILL: Yes, I know, but Henry's awfully jealous and … (*She starts laughing*)

TIM: And what?

JILL: He doesn't like artists.

TIM: He doesn't like … This farmer fiancé of yours doesn't think we're having an affair, by any chance?

JILL: (*Amused*) I wouldn't be surprised.

25

TIM: He's madly jealous, he doesn't like artists, and he
            thinks we're … I can see we're going to get on
            like a house on fire!

*JILL continues to be amused as TIM leads her through the
alcove. The camera follows TIM and JILL as they exit then
pans back to the dress on the model and then down to where
TIM has placed the parcel for HENRY.*

CUT TO: DAVID FORESTER's private study at a typical
Public School on the outskirts of St Albans.

The room is small, but comfortable. There is a mass of books,
newspapers, magazines, sports trophies, school photographs,
etc. DAVID's gown hangs from a peg on the door. There is a
telephone on a small table.

*DAVID is by the sideboard with a sherry decanter in his
hand. He is pouring himself a drink. TIM is lounging in one of
the armchairs, a glass of sherry in his hand.*

TIM: Well, so far as I can gather this detective chap
            seems to have asked us more or less the same
            questions.
DAVID: (*Turning from the sideboard with his sherry*) Yes.
            It was the other individual that puzzled me. What
            was his name – Colby?
TIM: Yes.
DAVID: I couldn't weigh him up.
TIM: He irritates me, he was so confoundedly polite.
DAVID: Well, obviously this card they talked about must
            be pretty important.
TIM: Yes. What did he say was on it?
DAVID: He told me it was a hand – possibly a girl's hand –
            holding a bottle of chianti.
TIM: Did Lewis ever send you anything like that?

DAVID: Nothing remotely like it. As a matter of fact it doesn't sound the sort of thing Lewis would send to anyone.

TIM: That's exactly what I said.

TIM drinks his sherry.

DAVID: Besides, I always thought those little sketches of Lewis's were, well – a private joke, peculiar to you and I.

TIM: Apparently we were mistaken.

DAVID: I don't think so. I think they're mistaken.

TIM: You mean, you don't think Lewis did send the card to anyone?

DAVID: I'm sure he didn't.

TIM: I wonder …

They sip their sherry.

DAVID: Tim, tell me about this man Briggs.

TIM: There's not much to tell. He was a pleasant sort of chap; North country, a pretty good businessman I should imagine.

DAVID: What was his business?

TIM: I don't know. I didn't ask him. He obviously does quite a lot of travelling.

DAVID: I gather, from what you told me, that he doesn't feel particularly embittered.

TIM: Embittered?

DAVID: Because of what happened. After all, if Lewis hadn't followed them down to Sorrento the accident would never have happened, and Alison would still be alive.

TIM: Did Lewis deliberately follow them to Sorrento?

DAVID: I think he must have done. Fenby told me the Gazette didn't know what he was doing down there, they thought he was still in Milan.

TIM: Well, Briggs doesn't seem to bear any ill feelings; on the contrary he speaks very highly of Lewis.

DAVID: (*Nodding*) It's a good thing. Let me get you another sherry, Tim.

TIM: No, I'm all right, thanks.

DAVID crosses to the sideboard.

DAVID: Oh, by the way, do you think you could put me up tonight?

TIM: Yes, of course.

DAVID: I've got an appointment in London tomorrow morning; if you can give me a bed it'll save me getting up at the crack of dawn.

TIM: Yes, of course, David – any time, you know that.

DAVID puts his glass down on the sideboard and moves the decanter to its original position.

DAVID: (*Turning*) Tim …

TIM: (*Looking up from his glass*) Yes?

DAVID: (*Quietly*) What does she look like?

TIM: Who?

DAVID: Alison.

TIM: Well, if the photographs are anything to go by I can understand why Lewis was so keen on her.

The telephone starts to ring.

DAVID: How old was she?

TIM: Twenty-seven …

DAVID shakes his head at the thought of anyone dying so young; he turns and lifts the telephone receiver.

DAVID: (*On the phone*) Hello? … Yes, this is David Forester … Yes, speaking personally …

DAVID puts his hand over the receiver.

DAVID: (*To TIM*) If this is who I think it is you'll probably hear some fireworks. (*Back on the phone*) Hello? … Yes … Oh, good evening! Yes, I got your letter … Well, you know, I really think under the circumstances you'd better have a word with the Head about this … Yes … Yes, I'm quite sure Charles explained it to your satisfaction. t's remarkable how he can explain things … No … (*A pause*) Since you ask me point blank, no I don't think the boy is a liar, but he's got a very smooth tongue … Well, perhaps you haven't experienced it like we have … (*A shade angry*) Frankly, he could talk himself out of anything!

TIM has been toying with his sherry glass, taking very little interest in DAVID's conversation; at this particular moment he looks up.

DAVID: (*Still on the phone*) He's as smooth as butter and he's got the voice of the nightingale … I will … I will indeed … Yes, I'll write to you. Goodbye!

DAVID replaces the telephone receiver.

DAVID: These parents! The boy's an absolutely smart-alec!

TIM: (*Quietly*) It's strange you should have used that phrase, David.

DAVID: Phrase?

TIM: The voice of the nightingale. Briggs said exactly the same thing when we were talking about Lewis.

DAVID: What do you mean? Lewis wasn't like that.

TIM: Briggs didn't say he was; he was drawing a comparison.

DAVID: Oh, I see.

DAVID suddenly looks at his wristlet watch.

DAVID: I think we ought to go down, Tim. I don't want to keep the Head waiting.

TIM: (*Smiling*) Oh, we've got the Head with us this evening!

DAVID: Yes, it's a sort of half-term 'do'. Oh, and Tim …

TIM: Yes?

29

DAVID: The Head loathes surrealism – so if you could be just a little luke-warm about it yourself this evening   …

TIM: (*Amused*) Leave it to me, old boy.

CUT TO: The living room / studio of TIM's flat.

Complete darkness. There is the sound of the front door opening and closing and then the sound of TIM's voice. The light comes on in the hall.

TIM: (*Off*) You can hang your hat and coat in the hall, David, then come through to the studio.

DAVID: (*Off*) Yes, all right.

TIM enters, switching on the main lights as he does so. He crosses to the drinks cabinet. The studio is exactly the same as in the preceding scenes, except that the dress and the photographs of Alison have now been removed as has the dress. DAVID enters.

TIM: (*Not turning*) I meant to ask you, who was that rather pimply old boy at the head of the table?

DAVID: Oh, he's one of the Governers; an argumentative old devil but quite good fun in small doses.

TIM: (*Turning with a decanter in his hand*) He made me laugh when he was talking about the Pre-Raphaelites …

TIM stops dead. He has noticed the change in the studio.

DAVID: What is it?

TIM puts down the decanter and walks slowly round the room.

TIM: (*Stunned*) The photographs … the dress …

DAVID: What photographs? What dress?

TIM: (*Tensely*) They've gone!

DAVID: (*Astonished*) You mean …?

TIM: (*Almost angry*) The photographs of Alison Ford –
            and the dress … You know what I'm talking
            about, David! They've gone!
DAVID: Oh, but surely …
TIM: They were here – here in the studio when I left!
DAVID: (*Looking round the room; quietly*) Is there
            anything else missing?
TIM: (*Stunned*) No … No, I don't think so …
DAVID: Well, surely someone wouldn't … (*With almost a
            little laugh*) Tim, you haven't imagined all this,
            have you?
TIM: What do you mean?
DAVID: Well, obviously no-one's broken into the flat so …
TIM: But someone must have broken into the flat
            otherwise how the hell did the dress and the
            photographs disappear!

TIM stares round the room and then dashes into the bedroom.
DAVID stands confused and somewhat bewildered.

TIM: (*Suddenly calling from the bedroom: tensely*)
            David! David, come here!

DAVID turns and crosses towards the bedroom.

CUT TO: TIM's bedroom.
TIM is standing in the doorway staring at the body of JILL;
she is on the floor – dead having been strangled. DAVID joins
TIM in the doorway.

DAVID: Isn't that the girl I saw here a week ago when …
TIM: (*Tensely*) Her name's Jill Stewart.

DAVID crosses and kneels down by the body.

DAVID: Yes, she's dead … she's been strangled. (*He rises*)
            Tim, phone the police …

TIM is staring at JILL; he doesn't move.

DAVID: (*Quietly*) Tim, do as I say – phone the police …

31

TIM: (*Still staring at JILL*) David … she's wearing the
              dress …

*The camera tracks in on JILL. She is wearing ALISON's
dress.*

CUT TO: The living room / studio of TIM's flat. About an
hour later.

*TIM is sitting in the wing chair looking towards the bedroom.
DAVID stands by the easel, a whisky and soda in his hand.
MAJOR COLBY comes out of the bedroom followed by
DETECTIVE INSPECTOR LAYTON. A plain clothes police
sergeant, carrying a flash-camera, comes out of the bedroom
and goes out through the alcove. COLBY looks at DAVID
then across to TIM.*

LAYTON:(*To TIM*) I'm sorry to keep going over the same
              ground, sir, but there are one or two things I don't
              quite understand.
TIM: (*Faintly on edge*) There's a great deal I don't
              understand, Inspector!
LAYTON: You say that the deceased is wearing a dress that
              doesn't actually belong to her?
TIM: Yes …
LAYTON: (*Taking a piece of paper out of his inside pocket
              and glancing at it*) A dress that belongs, or
              belonged, to a Miss Alison Ford?
TIM: (*Exasperated*) Yes, I've explained all that! I've
              explained about Norman Briggs, about the dress,
              about the photographs, about …
LAYTON: Yes, yes, I appreciate that, Mr Forester. But if the
              dress was here – on the model – when you left the
              studio earlier this evening then presumably Miss
              Stewart changed into the dress when she got
              here?

TIM: Yes, I suppose she must have done – but don't ask
           me why!

LAYTON: (*With the suggestion of a smile*) I'm not going to,
           sir. I'm going to ask you a much simpler question
           than that. Where is the dress Miss Stewart was
           wearing when she came to the studio, her own
           dress in fact?

TIM: (*Faintly bewildered*) I – I don't know where it is.

LAYTON: Well, it must be somewhere, sir – unless of course
           you're mistaken, and she is wearing her own dress.

TIM: (*A shade angry*) I tell you I'm not mistaken! That
           dress was here, on that model! It's the dress
           Norman Briggs brought, the dress that belonged to
           his daughter Alison!

The INSPECTOR glances across at COLBY.

LAYTON: (*Looking at the piece of paper again*) You've
           given us a very good description of this Mr Briggs,
           sir – but you didn't say where we could get in
           touch with him.

TIM: I don't know where you can get in touch with
           him!

LAYTON: Didn't he leave you his address?

TIM: No.

LAYTON: Didn't you ask him for it?

TIM: No.

LAYTON: Why not?

TIM: (*Really losing his temper*) It never occurred to me
           … I'm not a bloody civil servant, I'm an artist! I
           don't go round asking people where they live,
           what they do, who they are …

DAVID: (*Interrupting*) Tim! The Inspector is only trying to
           help you, there's nothing to be gained by losing
           your temper.

LAYTON: (*To DAVID*) Thank you, sir.

TIM: (*To LAYTON*) I'm sorry. I didn't mean to be rude.
            I apologise.
COLBY: (*Pleasantly*) Mr Forester …
TIM: (*Turning towards COLBY*) Yes?
COLBY: Was anyone else here when Mr Briggs called?
TIM: No.
COLBY: Did anyone else see the photographs and the dress
            – besides yourself, I mean?
TIM: Why, yes.
COLBY: Who?
TIM: Jill – Miss Stewart saw them.
COLBY: Anyone else?
TIM: Why, yes, David … (*He turns towards DAVID*)
            No, you didn't see them, did you, David? I told
            you about them …
DAVID: Yes, that's right.
COLBY: So in actual fact you're the only person who saw
            this Mr Briggs and, apart from Miss Stewart,
            you're the only person who saw the photographs
            and the dress?
TIM: Not the dress.
COLBY: What do you mean?
TIM: (*Nodding towards the bedroom*) We've all seen
            the dress …
COLBY: (*Thoughtfully; looking at TIM*) Ah, yes.
            (*Suddenly; quite pleasantly*) How long had you
            known Miss Stewart?
TIM: About three weeks.
COLBY: I take it you were very good friends?
TIM: It depends what you mean by very good friends?
COLBY: Well – you saw a great deal of each other?
TIM: Naturally, I was painting her. I don't paint with
            my eyes closed.

34

DAVID: (*Quickly*) What my brother means is that he's a professional artist and Miss Stewart was a professional model.

COLBY: (*Blandly*) Oh, I see. Thank you, sir. (*To TIM*) So that's what you meant?

TIM: That's what I meant, Major Colby.

LAYTON: When did you last see Miss Stewart?

TIM: I told you. This afternoon. She called just before I went out to St Albans.

LAYTON: Were you expecting her?

TIM: No.

LAYTON: Then why did she call?

TIM: It's her fiancé's birthday on Saturday and she asked me to deliver a present to him.

LAYTON: (*Surprised*) Her fiancé?

TIM: Yes. She was engaged to a farmer called Henry Carmichael. He lives at a place called Upper Netherington in Berkshire. I have a cottage about three miles from there. I was going down to the cottage at the weekend and Miss Stewart asked me to deliver the present to him.

COLBY: Why didn't she deliver it herself?

TIM: She said she was working at the weekend and couldn't get away.

COLBY: (*Quietly; apparently not very convinced*) I see. Is this Mr Carmichael a friend of yours?

TIM: No, we've never met.

COLBY: But you were going to deliver the present?

TIM: Naturally, I couldn't very well refuse.

COLBY: Have you still got the present?

TIM: Why, yes, of course! Unless …

TIM turns quickly towards the dais: the parcel is still there by the side of the armchair. He crosses, picks the parcel up and brings it down to COLBY who takes it from TIM, looks across

35

at LAYTON, then slowly examines it turning it over in his hands. After a moment, he unties the string, removes the brown paper wrapping, and takes out a wooden box. He lifts the lid off the box, removes a handful of sawdust, and extracts a bottle of Italian Chianti wine. He looks at the bottle then up at TIM.

COLBY: Rather an unusual birthday present, Mr Forester.

The camera tracks in on the Chianti bottle in COLBY's hand. We see the label; it is a typical Chianti label with the name of the Shippers prominently displayed. It is: NIGHTINGALE and SON.

END OF EPISODE ONE

EPISODE TWO

OPEN TO: The living room / studio of TIM's flat.

TIM, DAVID, LAYTON and COLBY are all looking at the Chianti bottle.

COLBY: Rather an unusual birthday present, Mr Forester.

LAYTON: *(Indicating the bottle)* You say that Miss Stewart asked you to deliver this to her fiancé – a Mr Henry Carmichael?

TIM: Yes, I've told you. He's a farmer; he lives at a place called Upper Netherington in Berkshire. I've got a cottage not far from there.

COLBY: And yet, I believe you said you'd never met Mr Carmichael?

TIM: That's quite true, I haven't met him. As a matter of fact, I know very few of the local people.

DAVID: My brother only uses the cottage for occasional weekends.

COLBY: I see. *(Pleasantly; to DAVID)* Do you ever use it, sir?

DAVID: *(Faintly surprised by the question)* I have done, yes.

LAYTON: Are you going back to at St Albans tonight, Mr Forester?

DAVID: No, I'm staying the night here. I have an appointment in Town tomorrow morning.

LAYTON: Is that why you came back with your brother?

DAVID: Yes. I told Tim about the appointment and he suggested that I stayed the night with him.

LAYTON: *(Nodding)* I understood you to say that you'd never met Miss Stewart, sir?

DAVID: That's quite correct: but I did see her on one occasion.

LAYTON: When was that?

DAVID: It was the day I heard that my brother – Lewis – had been killed in a motorcar accident. I came to

39

break the news to Tim. Miss Stewart was leaving just as I arrived.

LAYTON: I see. (*To DAVID*) Had your brother ever mentioned her to you – on any previous occasion?

DAVID: Not that I can remember.

LAYTON: You have no reason to believe that your brother and Miss Stewart were anything other than just – er – ...

DAVID: (*A shade too quickly*) No reason at all.

TIM: (*A shade angry*) If you have any questions about my relationship with Miss Stewart, Inspector, perhaps you'd be kind enough to address them to me.

LAYTON: (*Quite calmly*) Mr Forester, unless I'm mistaken, a great many questions will be asked about your relationship with Miss Stewart. My advice to you, sir, is to keep a civil tongue in your head and tell the truth.

TIM: The truth won't be difficult. I can't guarantee civility!

COLBY: I don't think you realise it, but you're in rather an unfortunate position.

TIM: Believe me, I realise it all right!

COLBY: I've had a certain amount of experience with artistic people ...

TIM: ... Oh, my God!

COLBY: ... And my experience is that, under certain emotional circumstances, they invariably say the wrong thing. The wrong thing can be dangerously misleading, Mr Forester – especially in a murder case.

TIM: (*Faintly exasperated*) Look, I have no wish to be either misleading or discourteous. The position is really quite simple. Someone murdered Jill

40

	Stewart. It's your job to find out who murdered her. You won't find it out by asking me a lot of damn fool questions!
COLBY:	(*Quietly; pleasant*) Then what do you suggest?
TIM:	(*Hesitant*) Well – first of all I suggest that you find out when she was murdered.
COLBY:	We know when she was murdered; she was murdered at approximately half past seven this evening. Incidentally, where were you at half past seven?
TIM:	I – I was on my way to St Albans.
COLBY:	In your car?
TIM:	Yes.
COLBY:	Alone?
TIM:	Why, yes …
COLBY:	(*Politely*) Any other suggestions? … Then I suggest that we continue this conversation tomorrow morning, at Scotland Yard.
TIM:	(*Quietly*) Yes, all right.
COLBY:	Nine o'clock, sir?
LAYTON:	Or is that too early for you, Mr Forester?
TIM:	(*Turning towards LAYTON*) I doubt whether I shall oversleep, Inspector.

CUT TO: The exterior of New Scotland Yard: nine o'clock the next morning.
A taxi drives up to the front entrance.

CUT TO: COLBY's Office, New Scotland Yard. Day.
COLBY is at his desk holding a newspaper up to his face reading it. INSPECTOR LAYTON enters with the Chianti bottle, label and cork which he puts on the desk. COLBY lowers the newspaper.
COLBY: Has Turner finished?

LAYTON:	Yes, he's checked the cork, the bottle, the label, the whole bag of tricks.
COLBY:	What about the wine?
LAYTON:	Well, that must have been all right – he drank most of it.
COLBY:	M'm. (*He looks at LAYTON*) Well, it looks as if we were barking up the wrong tree.
LAYTON:	I don't know. (*Indicates the label*) I'm rather curious about these people; Nightingale and Son ...
COLBY:	(*Turning; interested*) What do you mean?
LAYTON:	They're not in the telephone book and no-one seems to have heard of them.
COLBY:	(*Picking up the label and examining it*) That's curious, better keep checking.
LAYTON:	Right ...
COLBY:	(*Looking at his watch*) Forester should be here, it's nearly half past.
LAYTON:	He is here: he's in the anteroom. I saw him when I came down the corridor.
COLBY:	(*Nodding*) Let's have him in then.

LAYTON goes out. The telephone rings and COLBY answers it.

COLBY:	(*On the phone*) Hello?
JACKSON:	(*On the other end*) Major Colby?
COLBY:	(On phone) Yes ...
JACKSON:	Jackson here, sir. We've checked on the girl. She acted under the name of Alison Ford – her real name was Briggs.
COLBY:	Are there any details?
JACKSON:	Not many, sir. She was at RADA for a year and did six months in a weekly Rep. We're still checking on that.
COLBY:	Thank you, Jackson.

42

COLBY replaces the receiver. LAYTON returns with TIM.

LAYTON: (*To COLBY*) Turner wants another word with me. I'll be back later.

COLBY: (*Nodding*) Right.

LAYTON goes out again.

COLBY: (*To TIM*) Good morning, Mr Forester. Do sit down.

TIM sits.

COLBY: Inspector Layton and I have been going over the statement you made last night and there are one or two points …

TIM: (*Interrupting; with a faint note of sarcasm*) Which you don't quite understand?

COLBY: I wasn't going to say that, sir. I was going to say there are one or two points which you might care to alter.

TIM: Why should I wish to alter it? It was quite true.

COLBY: You still persist in your story about the dress, about the photographs, about the mysterious Mr Briggs?

TIM: There was nothing mysterious about Briggs. He was a perfectly ordinary chap who wanted his daughter's portrait painting.

COLBY rises.

COLBY: (*Shaking his head*) I don't agree. In the first place, if your story is true then Briggs' daughter was killed in a motorcar accident which was caused by your brother. Now Briggs knew that, he must have known it. Under those circumstances doesn't it strike you as being a little odd that he should ask you – you of all people – to paint the portrait?

TIM: Well, all I can say is that he did!

COLBY: (*With the suggestion of a smile*) Then he wasn't an ordinary chap, Mr Forester.

TIM rises.

TIM: What did you mean – my brother caused the accident?

COLBY: He was doing over sixty miles an hour on one of the most dangerous roads in Europe.

TIM: My brother was a very good driver!

COLBY: Not that good. Besides, he ... (*He hesitates*)

TIM: He what?

COLBY: (*Coming from behind his desk*) He'd had far too much to drink.

TIM: (*Angry*) I don't believe that!

COLBY: It happens to be true. I expect your brother heard about it.

TIM: David?

COLBY: (*Nodding*) He went out to Italy. It was pretty common gossip over there at the time of the accident.

TIM: (*Quietly; staggered*) Why, I can hardly believe it ... Lewis hardly drank anything at all.

COLBY: Nevertheless, on that particular occasion, he'd been drinking ...

TIM: (*Thoughtfully; puzzled*) Well, if that's true and Briggs did know about it, I must confess it was rather odd that he should have come to me for the portrait ...

COLBY: (*Quietly*) Mr Forester, I want to ask you three very frank questions – I hope you'll be equally frank.

TIM: Well?

COLBY: Were you having an affair with Miss Stewart?

TIM: No ...

COLBY: Did she have a key to your flat?

TIM: No.

COLBY: Did you murder her?

TIM: No, I didn't!

COLBY: (*A moment; nodding*) Thank you … Oh, Mr
           Forester, there's just one small point. Does the
           name Nightingale mean anything to you?
TIM: (*Taken by surprise*) Nightingale?
COLBY: Yes. (*He indicates the bottle*) It's on the Chianti
           bottle. Nightingale and Son.
TIM: (*Shaking his head*) I've never heard of it.
COLBY: I wondered, that's all.

CUT TO: The living room / studio of TIM's flat.
*DAVID enters from the kitchen and goes to the table as TIM
enters.*
DAVID: Hello, Tim! How did you get on?
TIM: It might have been worse.
DAVID: I was just leaving.
TIM: David, I want to have a word with you.
DAVID: Can't it wait, Tim? I've got this appointment at
           ten-thirty.
TIM: (*Facing David; bluntly*) What I've got to say
           won't take two minutes.
DAVID: What is it?
TIM: Was Lewis drunk?
DAVID: What do you mean?
TIM: The night of the accident – was he drunk?
DAVID: He'd had one or two drinks, I don't think there's
           any doubt about that.
TIM: Why didn't you tell me?
DAVID: What was the point? I knew it would only upset
           you, I knew … Oh, Tim, I knew what we both
           thought about Lewis …
TIM: But I don't understand it! Lewis wasn't a drinker.
           Something must have happened that night, David.
DAVID: (*Quietly*) Who told you about this – Colby?
TIM: Yes.

DAVID: I thought perhaps he might. When Fenby and I arrived at Sorrento the whole place was agog with it. Some said he'd been drinking steadily for two days; others that he'd had a row with some girl or other and was trying to …

TIM: Some girl or other? That could only have been Alison.

DAVID: (*A shrug*) I don't know. I suppose Fenby and I could have made enquiries – perhaps we should have done. But Lewis was dead and … Well, rightly or wrongly we decided to ignore the whole business.

TIM: Who identified the body?

DAVID: I did. (*Puzzled*) Why do you ask?

TIM: There was no doubt that it was Lewis?

DAVID: Good heavens, no – of course not!

TIM: When you came back you told me the car was completely wrecked and that Lewis and the girl …

DAVID: But it was Lewis all right. It was his car, Tim. The Bentley – TPE 246. Besides, both Fenby and I identified him. By the way, Fenby telephoned: he wants to see you.

TIM: I don't want to see him; I don't want to see any newspaper people.

DAVID: Tim, don't be silly! Fenby's a friend of ours, you've got to see him. Look, Tim, you're in a spot, it's no good rubbing the press up the wrong way – my advice to you is to tell Fenby the whole story.

TIM: Yes, all right, David.

DAVID: (*Looking at his watch*) I'm sorry, Tim, I really must go.

DAVID starts to go.

TIM: No, wait a minute! You remember the phone call you had last night, the one about the boy?

46

DAVID: (*Puzzled*) Yes?

TIM: You remember you used a phrase, rather an odd
            phrase I thought – the voice of the nightingale?

DAVID: Yes, I remember. You commented on it; you said
            that Norman Briggs had used it.

TIM: (*Nodding*) The name Nightingale was on the bottle
            …

DAVID: (*Puzzled*) What do you mean? Which bottle?

TIM: It was on the Chianti bottle that Jill Stewart gave
            me. Nightingale and Son.

DAVID: Well?

TIM: Rather a coincidence, isn't it?

DAVID: (*Thoughtfully*) Yes. Yes, I suppose it is, but just
            a coincidence, nothing else. Did you mention it to
            Colby?

TIM: No.

The front doorbell rings.

DAVID: Why not? If you think it's important you should
            mention it to him.

TIM: You've no objection?

DAVID: Good heavens, Tim, don't be silly! Of course not!

DAVID goes out to the front door.

CUT TO: The Entrance Hall of TIM's flat.

*DAVID comes out of the studio and opens the front door on
his way out. HENRY CARMICHAEL is standing in the
doorway. He is holding a newspaper.*

HENRY: Are you Forester?

DAVID: (*Surprised*) Yes …

HENRY: (*Striking out at David; intensely angry*) You
            swine!

TIM comes out from the studio also.

HENRY: Who the devil are you?

TIM: What's more to the point – who the devil are you?

47

HENRY: My name's Carmichael!

TIM: (*Surprised*) Henry Carmichael?

HENRY: Yes.

TIM: I'm afraid you hit the wrong man, Mr Carmichael.
          I'm Tim Forester.

HENRY: (*To DAVID*) I thought you said …

TIM: This is my brother …

HENRY: (*Suddenly, turning on TIM*) So you're Tim
          Forester! You're the swine that …

TIM: Now wait a minute!

HENRY: (*Tensely; trying to free himself*) You murdered Jill
          …

DAVID: (*Holding Henry; to TIM*) Who is this madman?

TIM: (*To HENRY; angry*) I didn't do anything of the
          sort! I know she was found here, and I know
          precisely what you're thinking, but you're wrong!

HENRY: Then what was she doing here?

TIM: Mr Carmichael, I'm just as bewildered as you are
          – even more so because I'm under suspicion.

DAVID: (*Releasing HENRY*) My brother's telling the truth.

HENRY: (*Indicating his newspaper*) It says here that Jill
          was a friend of yours and she frequently …

TIM: (*Tensely*) I don't give a damn what it says in your
          newspaper! I'm telling you the truth. I didn't
          murder Jill! Now, if you'll behave in a civilised
          manner, I'll tell you what little I know about this
          business.

CUT TO: The living room / studio of TIM's flat.

TIM, HENRY and DAVID are all facing each other.

TIM: (*To HENRY*) I suppose, like everyone else, you
          think I was having an affair with your fiancée?

HENRY: (*Bluntly*) Well, weren't you?

TIM: Did Jill give you that impression?

HENRY: (*Almost reluctantly*) No …

TIM: Then why should you assume …

HENRY: Look, let's face the facts! You're an artist; she was a model. She was found in your bedroom, so obviously …

TIM: (*Interrupting him*) All right, Mr Carmichael, let's face the facts! It's just possible that I could have had an affair with Jill. But I didn't. I didn't for a variety of reasons.

HENRY: Give me one!

TIM: (*Quietly*) I knew she was engaged to be married.

HENRY: Did Jill tell you that?

TIM: Yes, of course.

HENRY: All right, let's hear your side of the story.

TIM: I'd been dining with my brother at St Albans. We both came back to the studio. When we got here, we found Jill in the bedroom; she'd been strangled. She was wearing a dress that didn't belong to her; it was a dress I'd been painting, it belonged to a girl called Alison Ford.

HENRY: But why should she wear someone else's dress?

TIM: I don't know why.

HENRY: And how did she get into the studio?

TIM: (*Faintly; weary*) I don't know.

HENRY: Had she a key?

TIM: No, of course not.

HENRY: You say Jill told you about us – that we were engaged to be married?

TIM: Yes, of course. I was expecting to see you on Saturday. Jill told you that.

HENRY: (*Puzzled*) Jill did?

TIM: Yes.

HENRY: (*Still puzzled*) What do you mean?

TIM:	Jill phoned you and said I'd be popping over to see you on Saturday.
HENRY:	This is news to me …
TIM:	You mean to say she didn't phone you?
HENRY:	No, of course she didn't.
TIM:	(*Puzzled; a shade worried*) But – but she asked me to deliver a birthday present to you …
HENRY:	(*Astonished*) A birthday present?
TIM:	Yes, a bottle of wine – Chianti.
HENRY:	You mean to say Jill told you it was my birthday?
DAVID:	Isn't it your birthday on Saturday?
HENRY:	No, of course it isn't! My birthday's in September, and in any case Jill wouldn't send me a bottle of wine.
TIM:	Why not?
HENRY:	She knew perfectly well I never touch the wretched stuff. I'm completely TT.

TIM sinks into a chair.

CUT TO: The living room / studio of TIM's flat.

The telephone is ringing and Tim answers it.

TIM:	(*On the phone*) Hello?
DORKING:	(*On the other end*) Mr Forester?
TIM:	Yes …
DORKING:	Good morning. My name's Dorking. Reg Dorking. I don't think we've met but …
TIM:	(*Butting in*) What is it you want?
DORKING:	(*Laughing*) It's not what I want, dear boy – it's what you want.
TIM:	If you're a newspaper reporter, I've got nothing to say.

DORKING: (*Shocked*) My dear boy, I'm not in the newspaper racket! Whatever gave you that idea?

TIM: (*Irritated*) Well, who are you? What is it?

DORKING: Do you know the Bridge Road?

TIM picks up a cup of coffee.

TIM: (*Puzzled*) In Fulham?

DORKING: That's right.

TIM: Yes.

DORKING: Well, my place is on the corner of Chartwell Street. You can't miss it. Reg Dorking. Second-hand cars.

TIM: (*Annoyed*) Look, I'm not interested in a second-hand car, Mr Rorking.

DORKING: Dorking, dear boy. Dorking. D for devilment.

TIM: Well, whatever your name is I'm not interested.

DORKING: I think you'll be interested in this one, sir. It's a Bentley – Continental model. TPE 246 …

TIM: (*Staggered*) TPE 246 …

DORKING: That's right …

TIM: But that's impossible! My brother had a car with that registration number and …

DORKING: Nothing's impossible, dear boy. See you this afternoon. You've got the address. Bridge Road. Reg Dorking.

CUT TO: Outside of REG DORKING's establishment on Bridge Road.
TIM drives up to the establishment in his car; he gets out, glances up at the name, and walks towards the office.

CUT TO: REG DORKING's Office.
TIM enters and immediately finds DORKING who is smoking a cigar.

TIM: Mr Dorking?

DORKING: Yes.

TIM: My name's Forester. You telephoned me this morning.

DORKING: That's right, I did, Mr Forester. I did indeed. (*Indicating a chair*) Take a pew.

TIM: (*Still standing*) You said something about a Bentley – TPE 246.

DORKING picks up a piece of foolscap paper.

DORKING: (*Smiling*) Yes, I made a mistake. Got the wrong registration number. I've got a Bentley, but it's a '47. Done forty thousand miles. Immaculate. Just had a re-bore.

TIM: Look, I told you on the telephone, I'm not interested in a car.

DORKING: (*Grinning*) Then what are you doing here, Mr Forester?

TIM: You mentioned the registration number TPE 246. That was my brother's car; it was smashed to pieces on the Continent; he was killed.

DORKING: (*Staring at TIM*) Yes, I heard about it.

TIM: Why did you mention that number?

DORKING: (*A moment; takes the cigar from his mouth*) Would you have come here if I hadn't mentioned it? (*Smiling*) Sit down, Mr Forester.

TIM hesitates, then sits as does DORKING.

DORKING: Do you smoke?

TIM: Not at the moment, thank you.

DORKING: Are you in a hurry?

TIM: No, I'm not in a hurry, but I'd like you to get to the point – if there is one.

DORKING:	(*Nodding*) There is one. (*Looking at TIM*) I've got a friend who's got something he says you'll pay fifteen hundred pounds for – in cash.
TIM:	What is it?
DORKING:	(*Staring at TIM*) It's a postcard.
TIM:	What kind of a postcard?
DORKING:	(*Watching Tim; a shrug*) Just a postcard.
TIM:	Who is this friend of yours?
DORKING:	(*Smiling*) He's an old school chum. We were expelled together.
TIM:	Let me have a look at it.
DORKING:	A look at what?
TIM:	The card.
DORKING:	(*Shaking his head*) I've told you. It belongs to a friend of mine. I haven't got it. I haven't even seen it. I'm just the go-between.
TIM:	Well, what makes you think I'll pay fifteen hundred for it?
DORKING:	(*Calmly*) I don't think you will pay fifteen hundred for it. I told him so. I think he's nuts. But that's the message. "Tell Forester it's worth fifteen hundred pounds," he said. (*He shrugs*)
TIM:	(*Cautiously*) What's on this card?
DORKING:	It was posted in Naples and it's got a drawing on it. A bottle of wine and a girl's hand.
TIM:	I thought you said you hadn't seen it.
DORKING:	I haven't, dear boy. But I know what's on it. I like to know what I'm selling.
TIM:	Supposing I said I'd pay you the fifteen hundred – when could you get the card?
DORKING:	(*Looking at his watch*) Give me five hours.

TIM rises.

TIM: I'll phone you tomorrow morning.

DORKING rises.

DORKING: Okay, dear boy. Fair enough. You wouldn't like to see a nice Jag while you're here?

TIM: No, thank you.

DORKING: (*Stubbing out his cigar*) Maybe I'm crazy, I should be in the postcard business.

TIM: It sounds as if you are, Mr Dorking.

CUT TO: Hyde Park, later the same afternoon.

TIM is impatiently walking up and down by the side of his car. He is obviously waiting for someone. After a moment a police car appears and draws to a standstill near TIM. TIM crosses towards the car and as he does so the back door is thrown open for him to enter. He gets into the back of the car.

CUT TO: Inside the police car.

TIM and COLBY are on the rear seat of the car.

TIM: (*Tensely; on edge*) I thought you people were quick off the mark! It's over twenty minutes since I phoned you.

COLBY: Seventeen to be precise, Mr Forester. Anyway, what's all the excitement about? Don't tell me the elusive Mr Briggs has put in an appearance?

TIM: (*Shaking his head*) No, it's nothing to do with Briggs. You know that card you told me about, the one with the drawing on it?

COLBY: (*Interested*) Yes?

TIM: How much is it worth?

COLBY: (*Surprised*) How much is it worth?

TIM: Yes.

COLBY: You mean in plain L.S.D.?

54

TIM: (*Faintly excited; unable to control it*) Plain L.S.D.,
          Major. Pounds, shillings, and pence …
COLBY: You're pretty steamed up over something. What's
          happened?
TIM: A man called Dorking telephoned me. He's in the
          second-hand car business. To cut a long story
          short he says he can get me the card and he's
          offered it to me for fifteen hundred pounds.
COLBY: (*Surprised*) He's offered it to you?
TIM: Yes.
COLBY: (*Suspicious*) Why?
TIM: I don't know why, but he has!
COLBY: (*Quietly*) This is rather a development, isn't it, Mr
          Forester?
TIM: What do you mean?
COLBY: When I first mentioned the card, you said you'd
          never heard of it. You appeared to have grave
          doubts as to whether such a card existed. You
          suggested, if I remember rightly, it was hardly the
          sort of card your brother would send to anyone.
TIM: I still think that.
COLBY: But now you're offering it to me for fifteen
          hundred pounds.
TIM: No, I'm not. I'm simply telling you that a man
          called Dorking says he can get the card for me if
          I'll pay him fifteen hundred pounds for it.
          Whether I pay him the fifteen hundred or not is
          entirely up to you.
COLBY: When did you see Dorking?
TIM: He telephoned me this morning and I saw him this
          afternoon.
COLBY: Did he show you the card?
TIM: No; he hasn't got the card. He's just the agent; the
          go-between.

COLBY: You mean, he says he is.

TIM: Quite honestly, I think he is.

COLBY: Did he describe the card?

TIM: He says it was posted in Naples and there was a drawing on it: a girl's hand and a bottle of wine.

COLBY: What did you tell Dorking?

TIM: I said I'd phone him tomorrow morning.

COLBY: (*Nodding*) All right, phone him. Make arrangements to see him tomorrow night.

TIM: (*Looking at Colby*) And the fifteen hundred?

COLBY: (*A moment; shrewdly watching TIM*) We'll supply the fifteen hundred, Mr Forester.

CUT TO: REG DORKING's establishment on Bridge Road. Night.

TIM arrives in his car and drives through the lane of second-hand cars towards Dorking's office. Through a window DORKING can be seen at his desk. He looks up. TIM gets out of his car, looks round the yard – walks towards the office with a case in his right hand.

CUT TO: REG DORKING's Office.

DORKING is sitting at his desk. He finishes writing a letter and places it in his pocket. There is a knock on the door. He rises and opens the door. TIM is standing there.

DORKING: Come in, dear boy!

TIM enters. DORKING closes the door and returns to his desk.

DORKING: It's a pretty cold night, isn't it? Would you like a drink?

TIM: Did you get the card?

DORKING: I asked you if you'd like a drink?

TIM: And I asked you if you'd got the card.

DORKING: (*Nodding*) Sure … it's in the safe.

TIM: I'd like to see it.

DORKING: (*Amused*) What's the hurry, for Pete's sake! Is that the money?

TIM: Yes.

DORKING: Let me have a look at it.

TIM puts the case on the desk and opens it. It is full of money.

DORKING: Okay, fair enough.

DORKING goes to the safe.

DORKING: They tell me you're an artist. Is that a good business to be in?

TIM: (*Watching DORKING*) It depends how good an artist you are.

DORKING: (*Examining his keys*) Yes, I suppose it does. It must be pretty nice being an artist, a successful one anyway. What happens, do you wait for inspiration or just …

TIM: I didn't come here to discuss art, Dorking – I want that card.

DORKING: (*Faintly irritated, although smiling*) What's wrong with you? You're in a hell of a state!

TIM: This isn't a social call, it's a straightforward business transaction. Give me the card and you'll get the fifteen hundred.

DORKING: Look, don't get uppity with me, dear boy. So far as I'm concerned this is small beer anyway.

TIM: What do you mean?

DORKING: (*Pointing to the case*) I don't get the fifteen hundred, you know.

TIM: Why should you if it isn't your card?

DORKING: (*Moving towards TIM*) Mr Forester, there's something I don't understand about this. I've had a good look at that postcard. I'm no art

57

	critic, but that drawing isn't worth fifteen hundred pounds. It's not worth fifteen bob.
TIM:	Well?
DORKING:	Well, I'm curious. Why should you or anyone else pay fifteen hundred pounds for it.
TIM:	I should ask your friend that question.
DORKING:	I have.
TIM:	Well?
DORKING:	He's an oyster.

DORKING turns to the safe, opens it, takes out the postcard and closes the safe again.

DORKING:	I wish I had a nice racket like this ...
TIM:	I imagine you get by.
DORKING:	(*Shaking his head*) No, the second-hand car business is finished. As soon as you could get them off the ice the honeymoon was over. Besides, there's too many smart alecs in this business; so many slick operators, smooth talkers ... You know the type.
TIM:	I know the type, Mr Dorking.
DORKING:	Well, here's the card.
TIM:	(*Turning towards the attaché case*) You'd better count the money ...
DORKING:	(*Quietly; still watching TIM, a shade curious*) That's all right, I'll take your word for it. Can you leave the case?
TIM:	(*Hesitating*) Well –
DORKING:	I'll see you get it back all right. Here's the postcard.

Suddenly, unexpectedly, DORKING hits TIM and he falls to the floor. DORKING bends down and take the postcard and quickly leaves. The telephone rings. TIM slowly rises and answers the phone.

58

MAN'S VOICE:	(*On the other end of the line*) Hello … Dorky? … Hello? Is that you, Dorky?
TIM:	(*Weakly*) Hello?
MAN'S VOICE:	Hello, Dorky?
TIM:	What – what is it?
MAN'S VOICE:	I've got the address you want. It's 14 Sandown Gardens, Kensington … Hello? … Is that you, Dorky? Hello …

Suddenly we hear the click of the receiver being replaced at the other end and the dialling tone begin.

CUT TO: REG DORKING's establishment on Bridge Road.
TIM emerges from DORKING's Office onto the car lot. He walks to his car and opens the driver's door and stops dead, staring at the front seat. On it he sees the attaché case. He grabs it and opens it. All of the money is still in it.

CUT TO: COLBY's Office.
COLBY and TIM are in the office. The attaché case is on the table. COLBY picks up some of the notes.

COLBY:	You say you saw the postcard?
TIM:	Yes. I saw the drawing.
COLBY:	But not the postal mark or the address?
TIM:	No, the address was on the other side.
COLBY:	What was the drawing like?
TIM:	It was exactly as you described it – a girl's hand and a bottle of wine.
COLBY:	You think the card was genuine?
TIM:	(*Hesitating*) Yes … I think so.
COLBY:	But you're not sure?
TIM:	(*His hand on his forehead*) Frankly, I didn't examine the card very clearly. I suppose Lewis might have sent it to someone, I wouldn't like to say.

59

COLBY: You know, Forester, this is a very remarkable story of yours. First of all, you tell me that you can get the card for fifteen hundred pounds …

TIM: (*Depressed; irritated*) I didn't say that. I said that Dorking could get it!

COLBY: … We supply the fifteen hundred and the next thing we know is that you return without the card and with the fantastic story that Dorking knocked you out, vanished with the money, and for some obscure reason dumped it in your car.

TIM: Look, I don't pretend to understand this! I don't know why Dorking put the money in the car, I don't know why he knocked me out, but the fact remains he did!

COLBY: (*A moment, then:*) You said something about a telephone call?

TIM: Yes, when I came round, I was dazed and confused. The phone rang and I answered it.

COLBY: Who was it?

TIM: I don't know. I was in a hell of a state. I couldn't make out what he was talking about.

COLBY: Is your head still hurting?

TIM: Yes, it is. I've got the Home, the Light, and the Third all on the same wavelength!

COLBY crosses to a corner cupboard and takes out the dress worn by JILL.

COLBY: Mr Forester, I want you to take another look at this dress.

TIM: Well?

COLBY: You recognise it?

TIM: Yes, of course.

COLBY: It's the dress that Miss Stewart was wearing the night she was murdered.

TIM: (*Faintly exasperated*) Yes, I know. It's also
                the dress that Briggs brought to the studio, the
                one that belonged to his daughter …
COLBY: (*Shaking his head*) You're either mistaken –
                or your story isn't true.
TIM: What do you mean?
COLBY: This dress was bought by Jill Stewart from a
                shop in South Audley Street.
TIM: Are you sure?
COLBY: We're absolutely sure.
TIM: But – but that's impossible!
COLBY: The shop recognised a photograph of Miss
                Stewart and identified the dress. There's no
                doubt about it. No shadow of doubt.
TIM: (*Obviously worried*) In other words, you just
                don't believe me. You don't believe about the
                photographs, Briggs, Dorking … you just
                don't believe anything …
COLBY: (*After a moment*) Supposing you were in my
                shoes – what would you believe?
TIM: I don't know.

COLBY puts the dress on his desk.

COLBY: You see what I mean? Good night, Mr
                Forester. We'll be in touch.

*TIM leaves the room. The phone rings and COLBY lifts the
receiver.*

COLBY: (*On the phone*) Hello?
JACKSON: (*On PBX*) There's an outside call for you, sir
                – will you take it?
COLBY: Yes, please.

*We hear the background sound of a dance band through the
phone as the call is put through to COLBY.*

COLBY: (*On phone*) Hello?
LAYTON: (*On the other end of the line*) Major Colby?

COLBY: Speaking …
LAYTON: This is Layton …
COLBY: Oh, hello, Bill. Where are you? What's the
news?

*LAYTON is in a telephone kiosk at The Blue Circle Club. For
the duration of this conversation, we cut back and forth
between COLBY and LAYTON.*

LAYTON: I'm speaking from a place called The Blue
            Circle – it's a club in Kensington.
COLBY: Yes, I know it. Is Dorking there?
LAYTON: Yes, we tailed him here. He's in the bar at the
            moment.
COLBY: What's he like?
LAYTON: Personally, I shouldn't like to buy a fog lamp
            from him!
COLBY: Does he know you're on to him?
LAYTON: No, I don't think so. If he does, he's a pretty
            good actor. What do you want me to do?
COLBY: Pick him up, take him down to the local
            station and … No, wait a minute! Let's play
            this a different way. Tell him who you are and
            say you're investigating a stolen car racket
            and you'd like his advice. Play the whole
            thing up, make him feel important.
LAYTON: Right! And then what?
COLBY: My flat's just round the corner, take him there
            for a drink.
LAYTON: Okay.
COLBY: The address is 14 Sandown Gardens … Have
            you got it?
LAYTON: 14 Sandown Gardens?
COLBY: That's it. Give me twenty minutes …
LAYTON: Right!

CUT TO: The Entrance Hall of TIM's flat.
TIM enters. He switches on the light, takes off his hat and coat and crosses through the alcove into the living room / studio.

CUT TO: *The living room / studio of TIM's flat.*
TIM enters and switches on the room light. He crosses to the drinks cabinet, and then stops dead. The photographs of ALISON and the dress have been returned and are in exactly the same positions as before.

END OF EPISODE TWO

EPISODE THREE

OPEN TO: TIM FORESTER's Studio Flat.

TIM is staring in amazement at the photographs of ALISON and the dress which is back on the wire-model. In bewilderment, he crosses to the telephone, picks up the receiver and starts to dial a number.

CUT TO: The Drawing Room of MAJOR COLBY's Flat.

COLBY, DORKING and LAYTON are all present. COLBY is pouring whisky from a decanter into a glass. INSPECTOR LAYTON is sitting on the arm of a chair, a glass of whisky in his hand. COLBY adds soda-water to the drink he is mixing and turns towards DORKING.

COLBY: How's that, Mr Dorking?
DORKING: Splendid, dear boy.
COLBY: Would you like a spot more soda?
DORKING: (*Taking the glass*) No, no, that's just right. We musn't drown it.
COLBY: A spot more whisky, perhaps?
DORKING: No, no, that's very nice, ta.

COLBY mixes himself a drink and then turns towards DORKING and the INSPECTOR.

COLBY: (*Raising his glass*) Skoal!
LAYTON: Cheers!
DORKING: Here's to export!
COLBY: (*Smiling at DORKING*) It's very good of you to come along at a moment's notice, Dorking. We appreciate it.
DORKING: Not at all. Anything to oblige. I know what you boys are up against.
COLBY: Yes …
DORKING: The Inspector tells me you're investigating the stolen car racket, is that right?
COLBY: (*With a glance across at LAYTON*) Well – not exactly, Dorking.

DORKING looks at LAYTON.

DORKING: (*Nodding towards LAYTON*) But that's what you said. You said Superintendent Bradshaw here was in charge of the investigations and he'd be glad of ...

COLBY: (*Quietly*) My name is Colby. I'm not Superintendent Bradshaw.

DORKING: (*To LAYTON*) But you distinctly told me ...

LAYTON: Yes, I know I did, Mr Dorking, but we wanted to ask you certain questions and I thought that if I said ...

DORKING: (*Turning to COLBY*) Well, if you're not Superintendent Bradshaw, who the hell are you?

COLBY: I've told you. My name is Colby. I'm attached to the Special Branch.

DORKING looks at COLBY then at LAYTON again.

DORKING: (*A moment*) This is a bit of a frame-up, isn't it? You didn't get me here to talk about the car racket.

COLBY: No, I'm afraid we didn't, Mr Dorking.

DORKING: Well, what did you get me here for?

COLBY: You had a visitor this evening, a Mr Forester. We'd – er – like you to tell us what you know about him.

DORKING: Why?

COLBY: He's involved in a murder case so naturally we're rather interested in the gentleman.

DORKING looks at LAYTON and hesitates.

DORKING: There's not much to tell ...

COLBY: Is he a friend of yours?

DORKING: Good Lord, no, I never set eyes on him until yesterday afternoon.

COLBY: We understand he offered you fifteen hundred pounds.

DORKING: That's right, he did. Ruddy cheek.

COLBY: What for?

DORKING: (*Incredulously*) For a Bentley Mark 7. Fifty-one. Immaculate. Clean as a whistle.

LAYTON: (*Faintly surprised*) You mean, he wanted to buy a car from you?

DORKING: (*Regaining his self-confidence*) Of course. That's why he came to see me.

COLBY: (*Quietly; watching DORKING*) Tell us what happened.

DORKING: He answered an advert of mine – that was yesterday afternoon. He saw the car and was delighted with it. I was asking nineteen fifty; we had a bit of an argument and finally agreed on seventeen twenty five …

COLBY: Go on.

DORKING: He insisted on paying cash and said he'd bring the money tonight. Well, he brought it – but he only brought fifteen hundred.

LAYTON: You mean he wanted to make a deposit of fifteen …

DORKING: No, no, he wanted the car for fifteen hundred. He was trying it on.

COLBY: Go on …

DORKING: Well, to cut a long story short I lost my temper and let him have it.

COLBY: (*Politely*) The car?

DORKING: No. I clipped him one.

LAYTON: You – hit him, Mr Dorking?

DORKING: Yes.

LAYTON: You admit that?

69

DORKING:	What do you mean – admit it? I'm telling you, aren't I? Of course, I hit him! Wouldn't you have hit him? Fifteen hundred for a Mark 7, immaculate, clean as a whistle?
COLBY:	What happened after you hit him?
DORKING:	I just left him to cool off.
COLBY:	In your office?
DORKING:	Yes.
LAYTON:	What about the money?
DORKING:	I left that with him, of course. (*Suddenly*) Just a minute, dear boy! This fellow Forester isn't accusing me of ...
COLBY:	(*Interrupting him*) He's not accusing you of anything, Mr Dorking. But his story, and your story, aren't quite the same.
DORKING:	Well – what does he say?
COLBY:	He says you telephoned him, and he went to see you and you offered him something – for fifteen hundred pounds.
DORKING:	What do you mean – something? It must have been a car. I only sell cars.
COLBY:	Forester says you offered to sell him a postcard.
DORKING:	(*Incredulously*) A postcard!
COLBY:	Yes.
DORKING:	For fifteen hundred quid?
COLBY:	(*Quietly; watching DORKING*) Yes.

DORKING looks at COLBY then across at LAYTON.

DORKING:	(*To LAYTON*) Is he pulling my leg?
LAYTON:	(*Shaking his head*) No, he's not pulling your leg, Dorking.
DORKING:	(*To COLBY*) But this is fantastic, dear boy! What postcard's worth fifteen hundred quid?
COLBY:	Apparently the one you offered him ...

DORKING: But I didn't offer him one, I … Look, where am I supposed to have got this postcard from in the first place?

COLBY: We don't know. Originally it came from Italy. It was sent by a man called Lewis Forester.

DORKING: Forester? Is he any relation to the character we're talking about?

LAYTON: Yes, his brother. There were three brothers. Tim, that's the one you saw tonight. David, he's a schoolmaster – and Lewis. Lewis was the one who sent the card; he was killed in a motor car accident.

DORKING: (*Thoughtfully*) Forester … Tim Forester … (*A sudden realisation*) Is he the fellow that's mixed up in this murder case, the one about the model and the dress and …

LAYTON: Yes.

DORKING: Strewth, and I never realised it! What a damn fool! If I'd known that I wouldn't have had him on the premises.

COLBY: You still stick to your story about the car, Dorking?

DORKING: What do you mean – stick to it? Of course I stick to it, dear boy – it's the truth!

COLBY: And you know nothing about the postcard?

DORKING: Not a thing – except what you've just told me.

COLBY: (*Pleasantly*) All right. Let me get you another drink.

DORKING finishes his drink and puts the glass down. COLBY takes it.

DORKING: No, thanks, ta. I must push off. (*Looking at COLBY*) Fifteen hundred quid you said …

COLBY: (*Watching DORKING*) Yes.

DORKING: (*Amused*) Just for a postcard?

71

COLBY: Yes.

DORKING: (*Shaking his head*) That's an awful lot of lolly
            for a postcard. The most I ever paid was
            fifteen hundred francs and that was … (*He
            changes his mind*) Yes, well – goodnight,
            Major Colby.

COLBY: Goodnight, Dorking.

*DORKING goes out, followed by the INSPECTOR. COLBY
stands watching the door. After a moment LAYTON returns.*

LAYTON: Well – what do you make of that?

COLBY: It's an interesting story.

LAYTON: It seems to make sense to me. After all, if
            Forester was telling the truth why didn't
            Dorking take the money.

COLBY: I think he did take it and then changed his
            mind and dumped it in the car.

LAYTON: In other words, you don't believe Dorking?

COLBY: Do you, Inspector?

LAYTON: (*Thoughtfully*) He's a pretty smooth customer,
            but I've a feeling he's telling the truth.

COLBY: Then what's Forester playing at?

The telephone starts to ring.

LAYTON: I don't know, unless of course he's trying to
            convince us that …

COLBY: (*Lifting the telephone receiver*) Excuse me …
            (*On the phone*) Hello?

*For the duration of this conversation, we cut back and forth
between COLBY and TIM in his flat.*

TIM: (*Faintly excited*) Is that Major Colby?

COLBY: Yes …

TIM: This is Tim Forester. I've been trying to
            contact you for the last half hour.

COLBY: What is it, Forester?

72

TIM: Come round to my flat straight away – I've got
            something to show you.

COLBY: What do you mean?

TIM: Come round straight away – it's urgent!

*TIM replaces the receiver. COLBY still holds his receiver and
looks across at the INSPECTOR who looks puzzled.*

CUT TO: TIM FORESTER's Studio Flat.

*TIM is standing on the dais; he is staring down at COLBY
who is sitting in the wing chair facing the dais.*

TIM: (*Angrily*) What are you suggesting – that the dress
            and the photographs have been here all the time?
            That I deliberately concealed them? Shall I tell
            you what my first thought was when I saw that
            dress tonight? I thought, well now, at least, Colby
            will believe my story. He'll realise that I was
            telling the truth about Briggs and the portrait of
            Alison. He'll realise that I was telling the truth
            about …

COLBY: (*Quite calm, yet interrupting him*) Mr Forester, I
            didn't say I didn't believe your story, I merely
            said it would be a help – a considerable help – if
            you could also produce Mr Briggs.

TIM leaves the dais and moves towards COLBY.

TIM: (*Exasperated*) Well, I can't produce Mr Briggs,
            I'm not a confounded magician!

*COLBY looks at TIM, then rises and crosses to a photograph
of Alison; he stands looking at the photograph for a moment
and then turns.*

COLBY: (*Quite calmly*) Dorking says he knows nothing
            about the postcard; he says you offered him fifteen
            hundred pounds for a car. Is that true?

TIM: Of course it isn't true!

COLBY: (*After a moment*) No, I didn't think it was.

TIM: Well, I suppose it's something that you prefer to
            take my word in preference to Mr Dorking's.

The front doorbell rings.

COLBY: Forester, when you saw Dorking did he mention
            the name Nightingale to you?

TIM: No …

COLBY: You're sure?

TIM: Yes, I'm quite sure, but I tell you what he …

TIM stops, having heard the doorbell.

COLBY: (*After a pause: during which the bell continues*)
            Are you expecting anyone?

TIM: (*Shaking his head*) No.

*TIM looks at COLBY, hesitates, then goes out through the
alcove. COLBY looks towards the alcove, then turns and
crosses up to the dais; he stands looking at the dress on the
wire-model. There is the noise of the front door opening and
closing and the sound of voices. COLBY turns and looks
towards the alcove again. TIM re-enters. He is smiling and
obviously faintly excited. He is followed by NORMAN
BRIGGS.*

TIM: (*To BRIGGS*) My dear fellow, I'm absolutely
            delighted that you dropped in like this … Now let
            me get you a drink.

BRIGGS: (*Looking at COLBY*) No, no, if you don't mind,
            Mr Forester, I'd rather not. I've already had one
            or two and – (*A little laugh*) Well, I don't believe
            in over doing things.

COLBY stares at BRIGGS.

TIM: (*Enjoying himself*) Very wise. Very wise, my dear
            fellow.

*TIM looks at COLBY and grins, then suddenly picks up the
cigarette box and offers BRIGGS a cigarette.*

TIM: Perhaps you'd like a cigarette?

BRIGGS: No, thank you.

TIM: A cigar?

BRIGGS: No, thank you.

*TIM smiles at BRIGGS; there is a pause, then he deliberately
remembers that he has not introduced him to COLBY.*

TIM: Oh, I beg your pardon! I don't think you've met
          Major Colby.

BRIGGS: No, I haven't had that pleasure.

BRIGGS offers his hand to COLBY.

TIM: (*To COLBY*) Mr Briggs. Mr Norman Briggs.

COLBY: (*Impassively*) You surprise me.

BRIGGS and COLBY shake hands.

TIM: Mr Briggs, I wonder if you would do me a favour?

BRIGGS: Why, yes, of course. What is it?

TIM: Would you mind telling Major Colby why you
          came to see me – not tonight, but the first time.

BRIGGS looks at TIM, then at COLBY.

BRIGGS: (*Puzzled*) Why, no. (*To COLBY*) I came because I
          wanted Mr Forester to paint a portrait of my
          daughter – Alison.

TIM: (*Indicating the photographs and the dress*) And
          you brought me the photographs, and later – this
          dress?

BRIGGS: Why, yes, of course. That's why I called round to-
          night, to see how the portrait was going.

TIM: (*Smiling at COLBY*) Thank you.

COLBY: Mr Briggs, would you be kind enough to tell me
          who you are and what exactly you do for a living?

BRIGGS: (*Surprised*) Why the Dickens should I do that?

TIM: Major Colby has a habit of asking rather personal
          questions, he's attached to Scotland Yard.

BRIGGS looks at COLBY with new interest.

BRIGGS: (*Puzzled*) Well, what exactly is it you want to
          know?

COLBY: Do you live in London?

BRIGGS: My home's just outside Bradford, but I spend most of my time in London and flitting about the Continent, of course. I'm in plastics. You might have heard of us. Briggs and Taplow, St Albans.

TIM: St Albans?

BRIGGS: Yes, we've got a little place in Leeds too, but my partner looks after that side of the business.

COLBY: Where do you stay when you're in London?

BRIGGS: Usually at a hotel in Southampton Row – the Belvedere. It's not very posh, but they make me very comfortable.

COLBY: Is your wife still alive?

BRIGGS: No, I'm a widower – she died about four years ago.

COLBY: Any children?

BRIGGS: No – (*He looks at one of the photographs of ALISON*) We only had the one child – Alison – and she was killed in a motor car accident. (*Suddenly*) Anything else you'd like to know about me? Weight? Height? Blood pressure? Size of socks?

COLBY: (*Unamused*) You say you've got a business at St Albans.

BRIGGS: Well, it's between St Albans and Hatfield.

COLBY: Mr Forester has a brother at St Albans – David, he's a schoolmaster.

BRIGGS: Yes, I know, but we've never met.

COLBY: Didn't you meet him in Italy?

BRIGGS: No.

COLBY: He flew out there shortly after the accident happened.

BRIGGS: Yes, I knew he did; unfortunately, I missed him. I was in Sicily. It took them three days to find me and then I had to get back to Sorrento.

TIM: What a dreadful shock it must have been!

BRIGGS: It was. I just couldn't believe it. As a matter of fact, I didn't believe it, not for twenty-four hours. I thought there'd been some kind of mix-up.

COLBY: Why did your daughter stay behind – in Sorrento, I mean?

BRIGGS: Because of Lewis Forester. You see, Alison had met him in Milan and when he turned up at Sorento ... (*A shrug*) There was no keeping them apart.

TIM: What a terrible thing to have happened.

BRIGGS: (*Looking at one of the photographs*) Yes; she was twenty-seven. It's not very old, is it?

TIM: It certainly isn't.

COLBY: (*Quietly*) Mr Briggs, why did you wait until tonight before you contacted Mr Forester again?

BRIGGS: What do you mean?

COLBY: You must have read about the murder, the disappearance of the photographs.

BRIGGS: (*Looking at TIM*) What murder? What's he talking about?

COLBY: You know what I'm talking about. The murder of Jill Stewart.

BRIGGS: I haven't the slightest idea what you're talking about! Who's Jill Stewart anyway?

TIM: She was a model; she was found murdered in my flat.

COLBY: It's been in all the newspapers. You couldn't possibly have missed it.

BRIGGS: I haven't seen a newspaper for days, not an English one anyway. (*Faintly exasperated*) Look, I only arrived at London Airport just over two hours ago – what the devil's this all about?

COLBY looks at TIM.

77

TIM: You've been abroad since we last met?

BRIGGS: Yes.

COLBY: Where?

BRIGGS: Oh, all over the place. Paris. Rome. Milan. Naples.

COLBY: And you arrived back tonight?

BRIGGS: Yes, I've just told you. I arrived at London Airport at half-past seven.

COLBY: From where?

BRIGGS: From Rome.

COLBY looks at BRIGGS; it is difficult to tell what he is thinking. There is a pause.

BRIGGS: Don't you believe me?

BRIGGS takes his passport out of his pocket and offers it to COLBY.

BRIGGS: You'd better take a look at my passport, young man.

Still looking at BRIGGS, COLBY takes the passport. After a moment he looks down at it, turning the pages.

CUT TO: TIM FORESTER's Studio Flat. The next morning.

TIM is working on the portrait of ALISON; he continuously looks up in order to study the angle of the dress. There is the sound of the front doorbell and TIM puts down his brush and palette and turns towards the alcove.

CUT TO: The Entrance Hall of TIM's Flat.

TIM enters and opens the front door. HENRY CARMICHAEL is in the doorway.

HENRY: (*Faintly embarrassed*) Good morning, Forester.

TIM: Oh, hello, Carmichael!

HENRY: May I come in?

TIM: Well – it rather depends what sort of mood you're
          in.
HENRY: It's all right, Forester – no heroics, not this
          morning, I promise you.
TIM: Well, in that case …
HENRY: Thank you.
*TIM steps aside to allow HENRY to enter the hall, then closes
the front door behind him.*

CUT TO: TIM FORESTER's Studio Flat.
HENRY enters followed by TIM.
TIM: I'm rather glad you called this morning; I've got
          some news for you.
HENRY: Yes?
TIM: You remember, I told you that Jill wasn't wearing
          her dress – that she was wearing a dress that …
HENRY: That belonged to a girl called Alison Ford – yes?
TIM: Well, I was wrong.
TIM points to the wire-model.
TIM: That's the dress that belonged to Alison …
HENRY crosses and looks at the dress on the model.
HENRY: (*After a moment*) But isn't this the dress that Jill
          was wearing?
TIM: No.
HENRY: It's remarkably like it.
TIM: Yes, I know.
HENRY: (*Still studying the dress*) Well – has this dress been
          here all the time, then?
TIM: No, it was taken away by someone, (*indicating the
          photographs of ALISON*) … together with the
          photographs. Last night – whilst I was out – both
          the dress and the photographs were returned.
HENRY: By the same person?
TIM: Your guess is as good as mine.

79

HENRY returns to TIM.

HENRY: Forester, I called round this morning for two reasons. One, because I want to apologise for what happened the other day, and two because – I wanted to ask you something.

TIM: Yes?

HENRY: How well did you know Jill?

TIM: (*Annoyed*) Now look, we've been into all that before, we went into it …

HENRY: (*Stopping him*) No, no, I'm serious. I know she wasn't having an affair with you, but – was she a friend of yours?

TIM: (*Shaking his head*) No, not what you'd really call a friend.

HENRY: Had she worked for you before?

TIM: No.

HENRY: Then why did you pick her for this particular job?

HENRY indicates the finished sketch of JILL.

TIM: I didn't. About three or four weeks ago The Saturday Evening Mail asked me to do a cover for them, they suggested Jill. That was the first time we met.

HENRY: (*Thoughtfully*) I see. (*He looks at Tim; hesitates, then:*) Jill used to have an agent called Mary Hepburn.

TIM: Well?

HENRY: I wondered if you'd heard of her, by any chance?

TIM: No, I'm afraid I haven't.

HENRY: Jill never mentioned her?

TIM: If Jill had mentioned her, I should have heard of her, shouldn't I?

HENRY: Yes, of course. (*Casually; almost dismissing the subject*) As a matter of fact I think she retired

TIM: about six months ago. I seem to remember Jill saying something about it.

TIM: Then why are you interested in her?

HENRY: (*After a moment; facing TIM*) Mary Hepburn and Jill were very good friends, then suddenly they had a row. What the row was about I don't know – I don't think anyone knew – but I do know that …

TIM: That what?

HENRY: That … she threatened to murder Jill …

TIM: (*Astonished*) Threatened to murder her! Who told you that?

HENRY: Jill did.

TIM: Have you told the police this?

HENRY: No.

TIM: Well, why not?

HENRY: (*Hesitant; faintly worried*) It's six months ago and … Well, that's why I asked you whether Jill had mentioned her or not. I wondered if they'd been seeing each other.

TIM: I wouldn't know, but I certainly think you ought to tell the police about this.

HENRY: You really think so?

TIM: Yes, I do.

HENRY: I'm not sure; I've been in two minds about it.

TIM: What sort of woman was this Mary Hepburn?

HENRY: I don't know, I never actually met her. But I do know that she and Jill were very good friends; they'd been friends for years. Then suddenly, quite out of the blue as it were, they had this argument, or whatever you like to call it.

TIM: And you've no idea what it was about?

HENRY: No, I haven't.

TIM: You take my advice, Carmichael, and tell the police about this. After all, if she's innocent it can't do any harm.

HENRY: (*Interrupting him; obviously worried*) It can't do any harm; on the other hand, it is throwing suspicion on to the poor woman!

The front doorbell rings.

TIM: Yes, but you've just said she did threaten Jill.

HENRY: (*Perplexed*) Yes.

TIM: Well, that's more than I did and so far as I can make out I'm the principal suspect in this affair.

TIM looks at HENRY, then goes out through the alcove. HENRY, still faintly bewildered, turns and looks around the studio. He moves towards the photographs of ALISON. TIM returns with DAVID FORESTER. DAVID wears a black homburg and is carrying an attaché case and an umbrella. The folds of the umbrella are loose, and DAVID holds them together with his hand.

TIM: (*To DAVID*) You know Mr Carmichael.

DAVID: (*Significantly*) Yes. Yes, indeed.

TIM: I didn't know you were coming up to Town, David. You never mentioned it on the phone this morning.

DAVID puts the attaché case down on the table.

DAVID: No, it was a last-minute idea of the Heads.

HENRY: Well, I'll be going. Thanks for the advice. I'll think about it.

TIM: Don't just think about it, do it. Quite frankly, if you don't, I will.

HENRY: I don't think that would be a very wise move, Mr Forester. They'd probably think you had an ulterior motive. No, leave it to me, I'll speak to the Inspector about it.

HENRY nods to DAVID and goes out through the alcove, followed by TIM. DAVID stands looking towards the alcove, trying to adjust the folds of his umbrella. After a moment he turns and looks at the dress and the photographs. TIM returns.

DAVID: What's all that about?

TIM: Well, apparently a woman called Hepburn threatened to murder Jill Stewart.

DAVID: Recently?

TIM: About six months ago.

DAVID: Has he told the Inspector about it?

TIM: No. He didn't quite know what to do, that's why he came to see me.

DAVID: I hope you advised him to go straight to the police.

TIM: (*Quietly*) You heard what I said, David.

DAVID turns and looks at the dress and the photographs.

DAVID: Tim, I was amazed when you told me about this.

TIM: Yes.

DAVID: What did Colby say?

TIM: He didn't say a great deal, but I don't think he thinks I'm quite such an accomplished liar.

DAVID: I'll bet he doesn't. But what about Briggs – what made him turn up last night?

DAVID crosses towards the dais and the wire-model.

DAVID: Don't you think it's rather a curious coincidence that Briggs should turn up the same night as the dress and the photographs?

TIM: Yes.

TIM looks down at the attaché case on the table.

TIM: What's this, David?

DAVID turns and looks at TIM.

DAVID: H'm? Oh, it's some books I've got to take back to Foyles; they delivered the wrong ones.

TIM: (*Apparently accepting DAVID's explanation*) Will
            you stay for lunch?
DAVID: I'd like to, but I haven't time.
DAVID holds up his umbrella.
DAVID: Tim, have you got such a thing as a rubber band?
            This confounded brolly's flapping all over the
            place.
TOM: You'll find one in the dressing-room, right-hand
            drawer.
DAVID: Thanks.
DAVID goes into the dressing-room, carrying his umbrella.
TIM looks towards the dressing-room, then at the attaché
case; with his eyes still on the dressing-room he moves nearer
to the table. TIM hesitates, then picks up the case, obviously
interested in the weight of it.
DAVID: (*From the dressing-room*) Did you say the right-
            hand drawer?
TIM: (*Calling back*) Yes, the bottom right-hand drawer.
TIM looks at the attaché case again, then with a quick glance
towards the dressing-room, makes up his mind to open it. It
contains fifteen bundles of one hundred one-pound notes.
TIM is obviously surprised. He closes the attaché case and
replaces it on the table. DAVID returns from the dressing-
room adjusting a rubber band on the stick of his umbrella.
DAVID: That's better. I was beginning to feel like a
            Paratrooper.
TIM: (*Quietly*) How long are you staying in Town?
DAVID: I'm going back on the six-ten.
TIM: Well, drop in again if you've got time.
DAVID: (*Walking towards the alcove*) You might conjure
            up a cup of tea about half-past three.
YES: Yes, I will, David.
DAVID crosses into the alcove. TIM follows him.

CUT TO: The Entrance Hall of TIM's Flat.

DAVID and TIM enter from the studio.

DAVID: It's a curious thing, I can go without
                    breakfast, lunch, and even dinner at a
                    pinch, but the thought of missing my
                    afternoon cup of tea – Oh, dear me, no!

TIM: I'll see it's ready for you.

DAVID: All right, Tim. See you later.

*DAVID goes out. TIM closes the door and quicky returns to
the studio.*

CUT TO: TIM FORESTER's Studio Flat.

*TIM quickly enters from the alcove and crosses to the
telephone. He dials a number; his manner is tense and alert.*

MAN'S VOICE: (*On the other end of the line*) Brimley
                    Garage …

TIM: Is that you, Joe?

MAN'S VOICE: Yes …

TIM: This is Tim Forester. I want my car at the
                    front entrance – straight away!

MAN'S VOICE: Okay, Mr Forester.

TIM replaces the receiver.

CUT TO: REG DORKING's Car Mart on Bridge Road.

*TIM's car appears and drives past DORKING's, finally
coming to a standstill on a concealed corner. TIM gets out of
the car and strolls to the corner, from which he can get an
excellent view of the main entrance to DORKING's
establishment. He stands on the corner, then lights a
cigarette. As he lights his cigarette, a taxi turns the corner
and draws up outside of DORKING's main entrance. DAVID
gets out of the taxi, carrying the attaché case and his
umbrella. He pays the driver and walks towards DORKING's
office.*

CUT TO: TIM FORESTER's Studio Flat.

TIM's hat and coat are on the back of a chair, having obviously been tossed down. The front doorbell is ringing. TIM comes out of the kitchen carrying a tray containing afternoon tea. He hears the doorbell and glances towards the alcove; puts the tray down on the table, picks up his hat and coat and crosses through the alcove to the front door.

CUT TO: The Entrance Hall of TIM's Flat.

TIM enters from the studio and hangs up his hat and coat and then opens the front door. DAVID FORESTER is standing in the doorway leaning on his umbrella.

DAVID: (*Pleasantly*) Hello, Tim!

TIM: Come in, David.

DAVID enters.

CUT TO: TIM FORESTER's Studio Flat.

TIM enters followed by DAVID.

TIM: Let me have your hat and coat.

DAVID: No, it's all right. I can't stay very long I'm afraid. I've got an appointment at four o'clock.

TIM: Another one? You seem a very busy man these days.

DAVID: No rest for the wicked. (*He points to the tea tray*) That's very welcome, Tim. May I help myself?

TIM: Yes, of course.

DAVID: (*Pouring a cup of tea*) How's the portrait going?

TIM: Oh, it's a bit sticky. It's not really my cup of tea, you know.

DAVID: Nonsense!

TIM: (*Shaking his head*) No, it isn't. I've been doing this commercial stuff far too long.

DAVID hands TIM the cup of tea and then pours one for himself.

DAVID: Have you seen Major Colby today?

TIM: (*Sitting on the arm of a chair; watching DAVID*)
          No, I haven't. Why do you ask?

DAVID: I wondered, that's all. I thought he might have
          called round.

TIM: Why should he?

DAVID: Because of what happened last night …

DAVID indicates the dress and the photographs.

DAVID: … the return of the dress and the photographs.

TIM: (*Unable to conceal a note of unfriendliness*) He
          was here last night, I sent for him. I told you that
          on the telephone.

DAVID sits facing TIM.

DAVID: (*Smiling*) Yes, I know, but I thought he might have
          pursued his investigations as it were.

TIM: Well, perhaps he is pursuing them – elsewhere.

DAVID: Yes, that may well be.

TIM: (*Quietly*) David, you didn't believe my story about
          the dress and the photographs, did you?

DAVID: Yes, of course I did. But I'm jolly glad they've
          turned up, and Briggs too, it proves your story was
          true. When a story sounds as far fetched as yours
          did it's nice to have it substantiated.

TIM: Yes.

TIM stirs his tea; then looks up.

TIM: David, I saw a man called Dorking last night.

DAVID: Dorking?

TIM: Yes.

DAVID: Who's Dorking?

TIM: (*Watching DAVID*) Don't you know?

DAVID: No, I've never heard of him. Should I have done?

TIM: He's a second-hand car dealer.

DAVID: Well?

TIM: He telephoned me, and I went round to see him. He said he had the card that Lewis sent, the one that Colby was interested in.

DAVID: And had he?

TIM: Yes. He wanted fifteen hundred pounds for it.

DAVID: Good Lord! Did you tell Colby about this?

TIM: Yes, he knows all about it.

DAVID: And what did he say?

TIM: (*Still watching DAVID*) He was very interested.

DAVID: I'll bet he was! Anyway, I'm jolly glad you told him, Tim. If I were you, I should tell Colby everything.

TIM: I have done.

DAVID: Yes, but I mean – if anything else happens. (*Smiling*) Tell Colby everything. It sounds like a slogan, doesn't it?

TIM: Yes, and quite a good one.

DAVID: (*Smiling; reaching forward and patting TIM on the arm*) I think so. (*He puts down his cup*) Well, I must be off. I've got to see a man about a dog. (*Laughing*) No, I mean it; quite literally. (*Rising*) One of the college staff has a bull terrier, it bit the local postman, and it looks as if there's going to be a case over it. The Head insists on taking Counsel's opinion.

TIM: Is that what you were doing this afternoon, David – taking Counsel's opinion?

DAVID: (*Looking at TIM; hesitant*) No, I spent the afternoon at Foyles; we get our text-books from there. (*Suddenly*) Tim, I really must be going.

TIM: (*Quietly; watching DAVID*) Goodbye, David.

DAVID: Thanks for the tea. Sorry, I've got to rush off like this.

DAVID picks up his hat and coat and crosses into the alcove followed by TIM. There is the sound of the front door closing and TIM returns. He looks worried and depressed. He crosses to the portrait of ALISON, stares at it for a moment and then turns away and moves down to the table. He lights a cigarette; puts the lighter down on the table, hesitates, then picks up the telephone and dials. We hear the number ringing out at the other end.

MAN'S VOICE: Scotland Yard 230 1212.

TIM: Put me through to Major Colby, please.

MAN'S VOICE: Who is it speaking?

TIM: My name is … (*Suddenly; changing his mind*) No, it's all right, I'll ring later.

TIM quickly replaces the receiver. He stands, tense and worried, his hand on the receiver.

CUT TO: The Front Door of TIM's Flat.
PETER FENBY arrives and presses the bell push. FENBY is an educated man of about thirty-two or three. After a moment, the door is opened by TIM.

FENBY: (*Pleasantly*) Mr Forester?

TIM: Yes.

FENBY: I'm Peter Fenby.

TIM: (*Recognising him*) Why, yes, of course! I'm sorry I didn't recognise you.

FENBY: It's a long time since we met.

TIM: Come in, Fenby.

FENBY: (*Entering the flat*) Thank you.

CUT TO: TIM FORESTER's Studio Flat.
FENBY enters followed by TIM.

TIM: Would you like some tea?

FENBY: No, I wouldn't, thank you very much.

FENBY looks at the photographs and the dress.

89

FENBY: So that's it …

TIM: I beg your pardon?

FENBY: (*Pointing*) When were the photographs returned?

TIM: Last night.

FENBY: And the dress?

TIM nods.

FENBY: I bumped into Inspector Layton; I knew something had happened, but I wasn't sure what it was.

TIM: Well, that's it.

FENBY: Were you surprised?

TIM: Yes, of course I was surprised. Look, if you're going to write about this, I wish you'd make it perfectly clear that I'm just as bewildered as everyone else.

FENBY: I thought we'd already done that, Mr Forester.

TIM: No; every time I pick up a newspaper, I read that Jill Stewart was a personal friend of mine!

FENBY: Well, wasn't she?

TIM: No, of course she wasn't, she was just a model that happened to work for me. I employ models like – like a businessman employs typists.

FENBY: Yes, but she was found murdered, in your bedroom, Mr Forester. With all due respects that doesn't usually happen to a typist.

TIM: (*Irritated*) It doesn't usually happen to a model either.

FENBY: Have you any idea why Miss Stewart was murdered?

TIM: Not the slightest.

FENCY: Have you any idea why …

TIM: (*Interrupting him*) Look, I haven't the slightest idea why she was murdered, what she was doing in the bedroom, or how she ever managed to get into the flat.

FENBY: I see. (*Faintly embarrassed*) Well, I think I've got all the information I want. At least I know why the Inspector was so cagey.

TIM: (*Not wishing to be rude; but wanting to get rid of FENBY*) I'm sorry if I was rude; I'm rather on edge this afternoon.

FENBY: That's all right, it's understandable. But please remember I was a friend of Lewis's. I only want to help you, Mr Forester.

TIM: Yes, and that's very kind of you.

FENBY: If anything else happens or there are any further developments, I'd be awfully grateful if you'd let me know.

TIM: (*Trying to be pleasant*) Yes. Yes, I will indeed.

FENBY: The press can be quite a help you know, if they're on your side.

TIM: I'm sure of that.

TIM encourages FENBY towards the alcove.

FENBY: Give your brother David my regards next time you see him.

TIM: Yes, I will.

FENBY: (*Hesitating; with the suggestion of a smile*) And tell him not to spare the rod; I was dead wrong about Charles.

TIM: (*Repeating the message*) Not to spare the rod you were dead wrong about Charles.

FENBY: (*Amused*) That's right. Charles is a nephew of mine. His parents are abroad, so I'm responsible for him.

TIM: Does that concern David?

FENBY: He's his housemaster.

TIM: (*Quietly*) Oh, I see.

91

FENBY: And my goodness, I don't envy him! The boy's been staying with me for the weekend – what a little horror!

The telephone rings. TIM hesitates; he looks towards the phone.

FENBY: It's all right; I can let myself out. (*He smiles at TIM*) Goodbye!

TIM: Goodbye, Fenby …

FENBY goes out through the alcove. TIM stands looking towards the alcove, obviously a shade puzzled. The telephone continues to ring. After a moment, and with his thoughts still on FENBY, TIM picks up the receiver.

CUT TO: The Interior of a telephone box in a country lane. *MARY HEPBURN is on the phone; she is a good-looking woman in her early thirties.*

TIM: (*On the other end of the line*) Hello?

MARY presses button "A". For the duration of this conversation, we cut back and forth between MARY and TIM.

MARY: Can I speak to Mr Tim Forester, please?

TIM: This is Tim Forester speaking …

MARY: Oh, good afternoon, Mr Forester. My name is Mary Hepburn. I don't expect you've heard of me, but …

TIM: Yes, I've heard of you, Miss Hepburn.

MARY: Jill Stewart used to be a client of mine.

TIM: Yes, I know.

MARY: I'd rather like to see you, Mr Forester.

TIM: Why?

MARY: I – I want to talk to you about Jill.

TIM: My address is in the telephone book.

MARY: Yes, I know, but – I'm living in the country at the moment and it's rather difficult for me to get up to

	Town. I was wondering if you could possibly come out here?
TIM:	Where are you exactly?
MARY:	It's a place called Box Hill, it's near Dorking.
TIM:	(*After a pause; quietly*) All right, I'll come out this afternoon.
MARY:	(*Pleased*) Thank you.
TIM:	Give me your address.
MARY:	Actually, I live in a caravan; it's on a caravan site called The Garden of The World. Once you get to Box Hill, you can't miss it.
TIM:	Is there a name on the caravan?
MARY:	Yes – it's called Bella Vista. (*With a little laugh*) Sorry about that, it wasn't my idea.
TIM:	All right, I'll be there about half-past five.
MARY:	Thank you, Mr Forester.

MARY replaces the receiver. TIM looks at the receiver, then slowly replaces it.

CUT TO: Box Hill on the approach to the caravan site.
TIM arrives in his car; parks the car; gets out of it and walks towards the caravan site.

CUT TO: The caravan site.
TIM is on the site looking at various caravans.

CUT TO:
TIM is approaching a particular caravan. Steps lead up to the front door, which is slightly ajar. TIM approaches the entrance and walks up the steps. He knocks on the door; waits a moment and then knocks again. He looks around him, hesitates, then pushes open the door.

CUT TO: Inside of the caravan.

TIM enters and looks around, then stops dead, obviously surprised. The camera pans until it reveals an armchair in the corner of the main section of the caravan. ALISON FORD is sitting in the chair, watching TIM. She wears a dark dress and looks almost exactly as in the photographs.

END OF EPISODE THREE

EPISODE FOUR

OPEN TO: Inside of the caravan.

TIM enters and looks around, then stops dead, obviously surprised. The camera pans until it reveals an armchair in the corner of the main section of the caravan. ALISON FORD is sitting in the chair, watching TIM. She wears a dark dress and looks almost exactly as in the photographs.

TIM: Alison!

ALISON: Good afternoon, Mr Forester.

TIM: But – you're – you're, I mean, I thought you were killed in a car accident – you and my brother were …

ALISON: Lewis was killed, but – (*Shaking her head*) there was another girl in that car, Mr Forester.

TIM: Another girl?

ALISON: Everyone thought it was me, they took it for granted because Lewis and I … Look, there isn't a great deal of room in here, don't you think you'd better sit down?

TIM: (*Still bewildered*) Yes, I do. I do indeed. (*He sits*) I don't understand this. If you weren't in the car that night, then why … Why haven't you told anyone about this? I'm not the only one who thinks you were killed, you know. Your own father thinks so!

ALISON: (*Quietly; embarrassing him*) Does he, Mr Forester?

TIM: Why, yes! Yes, of course he does. He's been terribly distressed over this business.

ALISON: Are you sure about that?

TIM: (*Faintly bewildered*) Am I sure about what?

ALISON: Are you sure that my father's been terribly distressed?

TIM: Why, of course he has! (*A pause*) Aren't you and your father very good friends?

ALISON: No.

TIM: But he asked me to paint your portrait – why should he do that?

ALISON: I don't know why.

TIM: Does he suspect that you were not killed in the accident?

ALISON: (*Hesitating*) I think he might, yes ...

TIM: (*Puzzled, and even more bewildered*) Look, Miss Briggs – or Miss Ford ... er ...

ALISON: Alison ...

TIM: All right – Alison. Alison, I'm an artist. A simple, peace loving, sentimental artist. I like nostalgic music, children's crossword puzzles, simple books with happy endings and ...

ALISON: ... And nothing remotely complicated!

TIM: Exactly! Now would you mind telling me what this is all about?

ALISON: (*After a pause: looking at TIM*) Mr Forester, what's your opinion of my father?

TIM: (*Surprised, and faintly irritated by the question*) He seems a perfectly ordinary, amiable sort of chap. Why?

ALISON: A typical North country businessman, in fact?

TIM: (*Hesitant*) Yes ...

ALISON: That's what everyone thinks; that's what I thought once. (*Shaking her head; with a suggestion of tenseness*) But it's not true; it's not true, Mr Forester.

TIM: (*Watching her*) What do you mean?

ALISON: Until a few weeks ago I had had very little to do with my father. My mother died when I was a child and I was sent to boarding school until I went to Switzerland for five years, then to the Academy and into Repertory.

TIM: Go on …

ALISON: About six weeks ago my father wrote and asked if
          I'd like to go abroad with him. I was surprised by
          this because, although he made me an allowance,
          we were not – very close to each other.

TIM: I see …

ALISON: I needed a holiday, so I accepted. We went all over
          the continent. Paris, Brussels, Rome, Milan … It
          was while we were in Milan that I met Lewis.

TIM: Yes, I know.

ALISON: It was also while we were in Milan that I became –
          suspicious.

TIM: (*A moment; watching ALISON*) Suspicious of
          what?

ALISON: I'd always thought that my father was a
          manufacturer; that he was the principal partner in
          a firm called Briggs and Taplow.

TIM: Well?

ALISON: I discovered that that was just a front; that he was
          in fact engaged in – another kind of business.

TIM: What kind of business do you mean?

ALISON: I don't know, but Lewis did. (*She hesitates, then:*)
          My father thought that Lewis was making certain
          investigations; that he was attached to Scotland
          Yard.

TIM: Lewis attached to Scotland Yard? I've never heard
          such nonsense! My brother was a newspaper
          man, he'd been a newspaper man all his life.

ALISON: I'm only telling you what my father thought, Mr
          Forester. It might not have been true …

TIM: It certainly wasn't!

ALISON: Well, whether it was true or not, my father asked
          me to play up to him and find out what he was

doing in Milan. I refused; we had a row and I left
and went down to Sorrento.

TIM: Alone?

ALISON: Yes.

TIM: But I thought your father went to Sorrento?

ALISON: (*Nodding*) He joined me two days later; twenty-
four hours afterwards Lewis arrived.

TIM: Look, am I to understand that your friendship with
Lewis was engineered by your father?

ALISON: Our first meeting was, I don't think there's any
doubt about that. But something happened at that
meeting, that my father overlooked. I fell in
love.

TIM: (*After a moment; quietly*) I see.

ALISON: After two days my father left for Sicily and Lewis
and I stayed on at the hotel, I think my father did
this deliberately, in the hope that I'd find out more
about Lewis.

TIM: Go on …

ALISON: Suddenly, one day when we were in Naples
together, I made up my mind to have nothing
more to do with Lewis. It wasn't that I'd changed
towards him only I was frightened that he might
find out about my father and think that I …

TIM: I understand.

ALISON: The night the accident happened I was still in
Naples. I didn't go back to Sorrento because I
couldn't bear being near Lewis and not seeing
him. When I realised that everyone thought I was
the girl in the car I decided to … disappear.

TIM: Why?

ALISON: I was distressed, because of what had happened …
I wanted to be alone, and … I didn't want to have
anything more to do with my father.

TIM: Who was the girl in the car, do you know?

ALISON: (*Shaking her head; obviously distressed*) It must have been someone he'd picked up ... they said afterwards he'd been drinking ...

TIM: (*After a pause; quietly*) How does Miss Hepburn fit into all this?

ALISON: Mary's a friend of mine; she has been for years. When I arrived in England, I told her the whole story and she said I could stay with her.

TIM: I see.

ALISON: But what I don't understand, Mr Forester, is why my father visited you? And this girl – Jill Stewart – was she really wearing my dress?

TIM: No, I made a mistake. The dress was identical, but it wasn't the same one. Did you ever meet Jill Stewart?

ALISON: No, I'd never heard of her until I read about the murder.

TIM: (*A note of suspicion*) She was a friend of Miss Hepburn's.

Unbeknown to TIM and ALISON, MARY HEPBURN has entered the room.

MARY: Not exactly a friend, Mr Forester.

TIM turns and rises.

MARY: (*To TIM*) I used to run a Model Agency, and Jill was a client of mine. We were not friends.

ALISON rises.

ALISON: (*To TIM*) This is Miss Hepburn – Mr Forester.

TIM: (*To MARY*) You said on the phone that you had something to tell me about Jill.

MARY: That was simply because Alison wanted to see you. She was puzzled about the dress.

TIM: (*After a tiny pause*) Miss Hepburn, do you mind if I ask you a very blunt question?

MARY:	Not at all. When you're an agent you get used to very blunt questions, Mr Forester.
TIM:	Did you ever threaten to murder Jill Stewart?
MARY:	(*Taken aback*) Threaten to murder her?
TIM:	Yes.
MARY:	Why, of course I didn't! Who on earth put that idea into your head?
TIM:	Her fiancé.
MARY:	Jill's fiancé?
TIM:	Yes.
MARY:	I didn't even know she was engaged.
TIM:	She was engaged to a farmer called Henry Carmichael.
MARY:	Well, Mr Carmichael quite obviously suffers from hallucinations to say the least.
TIM:	(*To ALISON*) You said you were with Lewis in Naples?
ALISON:	Yes.
TIM:	Well, about a week after my brother was killed I had a visit from a Major Colby; he was interested in a certain postcard.
ALISON:	A postcard?
TIM:	Yes. Lewis sent it to someone. It has a drawing on it. A bottle of chianti and a girl's hand.
ALISON:	(*Surprised*) But I remember that card! I was in Naples with Lewis the day he posted it.
TIM:	Are you sure?
ALISON:	I'm positive. I remember it very well. I pulled his leg about the drawing. It was such an odd thing to send to anyone.
TIM:	(*Quietly: seriously*) Who did he send it to – do you know?
ALISON:	(*Puzzled by Tim's seriousness*) Why, yes. It was sent to a man called Fenby. Peter Fenby.

CUT TO: COLBY's Office. Early Evening.

DAVID FORESTER is sitting in an armchair. INSPECTOR LAYTON is standing by the desk and is on the phone.

LAYTON: (*On the phone*) Hello … Hello … (*He puts his hand over the mouthpiece; to DAVID*) I'm awfully sorry about this, Mr Forester. I can't imagine what happened to Major Colby.

DAVID: (*Glancing at his watch*) If I miss the six-ten there isn't another train until eight-fifteen and that means …

LAYTON: Yes, I appreciate that, but I would like you to see him before you leave. Hello? … Hello? … What the devil's the matter with this thing!

MAJOR COLBY enters.

COLBY: (*To DAVID*) Mr Forester, I'm terribly sorry. I do apologise. My God, what a meeting! I thought it was never going to end!

LAYTON: Mr Forester hasn't a great deal of time, sir – he's got to get back to St Albans.

COLBY: That's all right, he can take my car. (*To LAYTON*) Well, what happened? (*Pleasantly*) You don't look very happy, sir – was it an unpleasant interview?

DAVID: Not entirely.

LAYTON: Mr Forester's worried about his brother.

COLBY: Indeed?

DAVID: He followed me this afternoon; when I got back to the flat, he questioned me.

COLBY: About Dorking?

DAVID: Yes.

COLBY: Did you tell him?

DAVID: No, I lied. I said I'd never heard of Dorking.

COLBY: (*Smiling*) All right, don't worry. We'll take care of your brother.

103

DAVID: Does that mean you'll tell him the truth?

COLBY: If you'd prefer it that way.

DAVID: (*Nodding*) I should.

COLBY: All right, Mr Forester. Now, tell me what happened – tell me exactly what happened this afternoon.

DAVID: I left my brother's flat at about half past one and picked up a taxi on the corner of Sloane Street …

CUT TO: *David arriving at DORKING's in a taxi.*

DAVID'S VOICE:It was about a quarter to two when I arrived at Dorking's.

CUT TO: DORKING's Office.

DAVID'S VOICE:Dorking had just finished lunch and he was sitting behind his desk; when I told him the reason for my visit, he picked up a catalogue and tossed it towards me.

DORKING picks up a catalogue and tosses it across his desk.

DORKING: I'm in the motor car business, old boy. If it's postcards you want, there's a stationers on the next corner.

DAVID: It's not postcards I want, Mr Dorking – it's a particular postcard.

DORKING: And what makes you think I've got this particular postcard?

DAVID: You told my brother you'd got it, you said you'd sell it to him for fifteen hundred pounds.

DORKING: Who told you that?

DAVID: Tim – my brother.

DORKING: He's nuts!

DAVID: (*Quietly*) You telephoned the wrong one, Dorking.

DORKING: What do you mean?

DAVID: You picked the wrong Mr Forester. There's two of us. Tim – the artist. David – the schoolmaster, that's me.

DORKING: What is this, old boy? Happy families? Listen, I don't know anything about a postcard. If you don't get the hell out of here, I'll phone the police.

DAVID: (*Unperturbed*) All right – go ahead. Tell them my name is Forester and I'm offering you fifteen hundred pounds for a postcard.

DORKING: You're a pretty calm customer; you're not my idea of a schoolmaster.

DAVID: Perhaps you've got the wrong idea.

DORKING: (*Eyeing DAVID*) I shouldn't like you to teach my kids.

DAVID: I'm delighted to hear it.

DORKING: You're too smooth, old boy – too glib for my liking. You've got the – what do you call it?

DAVID: The voice of the nightingale?

DORKING: Yes … Yes, that's it … (*Indicating DAVID's attaché case*) How much have you got in there?

DAVID: Fifteen hundred.

DORKING: It's not enough.

DAVID: It's all you're getting, old boy.

DORKING: Okay, teacher …

DAVID'S VOICE: He handed me the card and took the money: he didn't even bother to count it.

CUT TO: COLBY's Office. As before.

COLBY: Where is the card?

LAYTON:	I sent it straight down to Hooper.
COLBY:	Have you had a report?
LAYTON:	No, not yet.
DAVID:	Look, I did what you wanted, Major Colby, but I still don't see the point of it.

DAVID rises.

COLBY:	The point is, in our opinion, Dorking's simply a go-between. He'll pass that money on to someone else. We want to know who.
DAVID:	But how will you find out?
LAYTON:	(*Smiling*) Don't worry, we'll find out.
DAVID:	Inspector, when you asked me to do this for you, I said I'd do it on one condition. You remember what that condition was?
INSPECTOR:	(*Quietly*) Yes, I remember.
COLBY:	(*Pleasantly; to DAVID*) I think the Inspector promised to tell you what was on the card, Mr Forester.
DAVID:	(*Looking at COLBY*) Yes, he did.
COLBY:	Well, there's a drawing: a bottle of chianti and …
DAVID:	(*Interrupting him*) Yes, I know all about the drawing, but what else is on the card?
COLBY:	(*After a tiny pause*) If it's the correct card, the one we're looking for, then after certain treatment it … should reveal a list of names.
DAVID:	(*Quietly, surprised*) A list of names?
COLBY:	Yes.
DAVID:	(*Apparently disappointed*) Is that all?
COLBY:	(*Smiling*) That's all, Mr Forester.
DAVID:	(*Suddenly amused*) Good heavens, I thought at least there'd be a map and details of hidden treasure!

The telephone rings and LAYTON answers it.

LAYTON: (*On the phone*) Hello?

HOOPER: (*On the other end; an educated voice*) Inspector?

LAYTON: Yes?

HOOPER: This is Hooper. We've made the test, sir. It's negative.

LAYTON: Thank you, Hooper.

LAYTON replaces the telephone and turns to COLBY.

LAYTON: It's the wrong card.

CUT TO: COLBY's Office. Half an hour later.

COLBY is sitting at his desk. LAYTON enters.

LAYTON: Forester's here, he says he'd like to see you.

COLBY: But I thought he left half an hour ago?

LAYTON: (*Shaking his head*) This is the other one – the artist chap.

COLBY: Oh …

LAYTON: He seems pretty steamed up about something.

COLBY: (*Rising from his desk; smiling*) Yes, and you know what it is.

LAYTON: You think he's come to tell us about his brother and Dorking?

COLBY: (*Nodding*) That's it all right. Send him in. (*Suddenly*) Oh, Inspector – I meant to ask you. Whose keeping an eye on Dorking?

LAYTON: Reed.

COLBY: Is that the young fellow they call 'Hunch' Reed?

LAYTON: That's the chap; and his hunches are worth listening to.

LAYTON goes out. COLBY rises and looks out of the window.
As LAYTON returns with TIM, COLBY turns back.

COLBY: Good evening, Mr Forester. (*Indicating a chair*) Won't you sit down?

TIM: (*Ignoring the chair*) I've got some news for you, Major Colby.

COLBY: Indeed?

TIM: That postcard you're so interested in.

COLBY: Yes?

TIM: It was posted in Naples and sent to a man called Peter Fenby.

LAYTON: Peter Fenby?

TIM: Yes.

LAYTON: He's on the London Gazette.

TIM: That's right. He was a friend of Lewis's. He flew out to Italy with my brother David.

LAYTON: But we've seen Fenby; we questioned him about the card. As a matter of fact, he was the first person we saw.

TIM: And what did he say?

LAYTON: He said he knew nothing about it.

TIM: (*Faintly aggressive*) Then he's lying!

COLBY: (*Quietly*) Sit down, Mr Forester.

Somewhat reluctantly, TIM sits.

COLBY: This is an interesting theory of yours. Why haven't you told us about it before?

TIM: This isn't a theory; it's a fact. The card was posted to Peter Fenby.

COLBY: How do you know?

TIM: (*A moment*) Alison Ford told me.

LAYTON: Alison Ford?

TIM: Yes.

LAYTON: You mean the girl in the car – the girl that was killed?

TIM: Yes – except that she wasn't killed.

COLBY: When did you see Miss Ford?

TIM: This afternoon.

COLBY: Where?

TIM: (*Hesitant*) She's staying with a friend. Alison read about the murder and the dress and she asked the friend to telephone me.

LAYTON: (*Tensely; with authority*) Where is this girl?

TIM: I've arranged for you to see her tomorrow afternoon.

LAYTON: (*Indignantly*) You've arranged for us to see her!

TIM: Yes.

LAYTON: If Miss Ford's alive we're seeing her tonight – now!

TIM: (*Quietly*) You're seeing Miss Ford tomorrow afternoon, Inspector – at my flat – at three o'clock – (*He shakes his head*) not before.

COLBY: (*Faintly amused*) Does Mr Briggs know that his daughter's alive?

TIM: (*Evasively*) I haven't told him, if that's what you're thinking.

COLBY: You say that Miss Briggs – or Miss Ford – told you that the card was sent to Peter Fenby?

TIM: Yes; she remembers the card. She was with Lewis the day he posted it.

COLBY picks up the phone.

VOICE: (*On the other end of the phone*) Yes, sir?

COLBY: (*On the phone*) Get me a man called Fenby – Peter Fenby. He's on the London Gazette.

COLBY replaces the receiver.

COLBY: (*To TIM*) Well, for an artist you spring some pretty dramatic surprises, Mr Forester. I thought you were going to tell us something quite different.

TIM: What exactly?

COLBY: I thought you were going to tell us that your brother went to see Dorking this afternoon.

TIM: (*Apparently surprised*) My brother went to see Dorking this afternoon?

109

COLBY: Yes.

LAYTON: You followed him there, Mr Forester, we know all about it.

COLBY: I sent your brother to Dorking's.

TIM: You sent him?

COLBY: Yes. He's been helping us.

TIM: And I thought …

COLBY: I had a pretty shrewd suspicion that if you'd said the right thing the other night Dorking would have handed over the card.

TIM: And did my brother say the right thing?

COLBY: Yes.

TIM: Then presumably you've got the card.

COLBY: We've got Mr Dorking's card – unfortunately it isn't the right one.

The telephone rings.

COLBY: (*To TIM*) When Fenby gets here, I'd like you to talk to him. Tell him there's been a new development and you thought he might be interested. Ask him to call round and see you sometime tonight.

TIM: Do I get a pension on this job?

COLBY: (*Smiling*) You do if we get the card, Mr Forester.

CUT TO: PETER FENBY's Office. Evening.

PETER FENBY is sitting at his desk. He is talking on the telephone. For the duration of this conversation, we cut back and forth between FENBY and TIM in COLBY's office.

FENBY: (*On the phone*) Hello?

TIM: (*On the other end*) Is that Peter Fenby?

FENBY: Speaking …

TIM: This is Tim Forester.

FENBY: Oh, hello, Forester!

110

TIM: Fenby, when I saw you the other day, I believe I
          promised to let you know if there were any further
          developments.
FENBY: That's right, you did.
TIM: Well, something's happened – something I think
          you ought to know about.
FENBY: All right, old boy. Carry on.
TIM: No, I can't tell you on the phone, Fenby, I'd like
          to see you. Can you call round sometime?
FENBY: Yes, why not? When would you suggest?
TIM: Well, tonight – seven o'clock. How would that
          suit you?
FENBY: That's fine.
TIM: All right, Fenby – I'll see you then.
FENBY: (*Suddenly*) Oh, Forester ...
TIM: Yes?
FENBY: (*Quite casual*) Are you speaking from home?
TIM: (*A moment's hesitation*) Why, yes. Why do you
          ask?
FENBY: (*Vaguely*) I wondered, that's all. See you about
          seven.

CUT TO: TIM's Studio Flat. Later the same evening.
*TIM, LAYTON and COLBY are all waiting for FENBY to
arrive.*
LAYTON:It's after eight. I doubt whether we shall see Mr
          Fenby this evening.
COLBY: Yes, I'm beginning to doubt it.
LAYTON:(*To TIM*) You said – he asked you whether you
          were speaking from home?
TIM: Yes.
LAYTON: (*Nodding*) I'll bet a fiver he knew you weren't.
COLBY: He probably checked this number the moment you
          rang off.

TIM: Yes, I hadn't thought of that.

COLBY: Have you got his private address?

TIM: No, I haven't. But I expect he's in the book, under the table there.

COLBY reaches down and picks up the book TIM is referring to.

COLBY: (*Turning the pages of the book*) How well did your brother know Fenby, Mr Forester?

TIM: Oh, I think they were pretty close friends. They'd worked together for many years.

COLBY: Is your other brother – David – a friend of his?

TIM: (*Hesitating*) Not really.

LAYTON: When did you first meet him?

TIM: Oh, I should say about two or three years ago. My brother – Lewis – gave a cocktail party. Fenby made rather a beeline for me, he wanted me to illustrate some articles he was writing.

LAYTON: Did you illustrate them?

TIM: No.

COLBY: (*Looking up from the book*) Apparently, he's not in the book.

The doorbell rings. TIM, COLBY and LAYTON all look at each other. COLBY indicates for TIM to go and answer the door.

CUT TO: The Entrance Hall of TIM's flat.

TIM enters from the studio and opens the door. HENRY CARMICHAEL is standing in the doorway.

TIM: Come in, Carmichael!

HENRY: Are you alone?

TIM: No, Inspector Layton's here and Major Colby.

HENRY: (*Surprised; a note of tenseness in his voice*) Inspector … (*Quietly, taking hold of TIM's lapel*)

	Have you told the Inspector what I told you this morning?
TIM:	What was that?
HENRY:	About Mary Hepburn …
TIM:	No, as a matter of fact, I haven't.
HENRY:	Don't tell him, Forester. I was wrong. It wasn't Mary Hepburn that threatened Jill, it was …
TIM:	(*Watching HENRY*) But you distinctly told me …
HENRY:	Yes, I know I did, but I was mistaken, completely mistaken, it was someone else. (*With a nervous glance towards the studio*) I'll tell you later, Forester – not now.

CUT TO: TIM's Studio Flat. Later the same evening.
TIM enters, followed by HENRY CARMICHAEL. They join COLBY and INSPECTOR LAYTON.

TIM:	(*To LAYTON and COLBY*) I'm afraid it's not the gentleman we're expecting.
LAYTON:	(*To HENRY*) Good evening, Mr Carmichael.
HENRY:	Good evening, Inspector.
TIM:	I think you know Major Colby?
HENRY:	Yes, we have met. (*To TIM*) I'm sorry, barging in like this, Forester. I suppose I ought to have telephoned you …
TIM:	That's all right.
COLBY:	Is this a private matter, because if it is …
HENRY:	(*Thinking fast*) No, no, no – it's nothing. It's just that … (*To TIM*) Forester, I hope you don't think this is an impertinence, but I was wondering if I could buy that portrait off you?
TIM:	Which portrait?
HENRY:	The one of Jill.
TIM:	I'm afraid you'll have to ask the magazine about that, they own the copyright.

HENRY: Oh, I see. I never thought of that.

COLBY: (*Quietly; watching HENRY*) Why do you want the portrait, Mr Carmichael?

HENRY: (*A shade irritated*) Because I haven't got one of Jill. I haven't even got a decent photograph.

TIM: (*After a moment*) I've got one or two sketches if you'd like to see them?

HENRY: Yes, I would.

TIM: They're just roughs, of course, but –

HENRY: I'd love to see them, Mr Forester.

TIM goes off to find the sketches.

COLBY: Mr Carmichael, when you came to Scotland Yard the other day you told us that you were a teetotaller.

HENRY: Did I?

COLBY: Yes. We told you about the bottle of Chianti – the supposed birthday present – and you said that not only was is <u>not</u> your birthday, but you were a teetotaller. In short, you inferred that Miss Stewart would never have given you a bottle of wine even if it had been your birthday.

HENRY: Well?

COLBY: Well, Mr Carmichael – does the name Pandora mean anything to you?

HENRY: (*Hesitant*) Pandora?

COLBY: Yes.

HENRY: (*After a moment; watching COLBY*) Isn't it a club in South Audley Street?

COLBY: It is.

HENRY: Well?

COLBY: Well – aren't you a member?

HENRY: (*Faintly embarrassed*) Yes, I suppose … I am.

COLBY: What do you mean – you suppose you are? Either you're a member or you're not a member?

114

HENRY: I – I am a member.

COLBY: And a very unique one, unless I'm mistaken.

HENRY: What do you mean?

COLBY: I doubt whether the Pandora has many teetotallers.

HENRY: Look, I only joined the Pandora because Jill asked me to. I'm not interested in that sort of place.

COLBY: (*Quietly*) You were there two nights ago, Mr Carmichael.

HENRY: (*Irritated*) Was I?

COLBY: (*Nodding; quite pleasant*) You were. You had two pink gins and a dry martini.

HENRY: Look here, have you been making enquiries about me?

COLBY: Of course. (*Smiling*) It's my job to make enquiries about people, that's what I'm paid for.

HENRY: (*After a moment*) It's perfectly true I was at the Pandora. I – I was lonely … I felt worried … and very depressed.

COLBY: So you had two pink gins and a dry martini?

HENRY: Yes.

TIM returns with two sketches of JILL in his hands.

TIM: (*Crossing to HENRY with the sketches*) I think these two are the best …

HENRY: Thank you. (*HENRY looks at the two sketches*) I like this one … It's very good indeed.

TIM: Well, you can have that if you like.

HENRY: Thank you, Mr Forester. It's very kind of you. I appreciate it. Well – er – Goodnight, Inspector.

LAYTON: Goodnight, Mr Carmichael.

COLBY: (*To HENRY, pleasantly*) Have you got a car, sir?

HENRY: Er – yes.

COLBY: Which way are you going?

HENRY: (*He isn't sure what to say*) Well – er – actually I'm going to Knightsbridge.

COLBY: Oh, splendid! Perhaps you'd drop me in Piccadilly?

HENRY: Yes. Yes, of course.

COLBY: That's very kind of you. (*To LAYTON*) I'll find the address we want and contact you later.

LAYTON: Yes, all right, Major.

HENRY: (*To TIM*) Thank you again for the sketch, Mr Forester.

The telephone starts to ring.

TIM: (*Crossing to the telephone*) That's all right.

TIM answers the telephone.

TIM: (*On the phone*) Hello?

REED: (*On the other end of the phone*) Is that Mr Forester?

For the duration of this conversation, we cut back and forth between TIM and DETECTIVE SERGEANT REED who is in a telephone box.

TIM: Yes?

REED: This is Detective Sergeant Reed, could I speak to the Inspector, sir?

TIM: Yes, certainly. (*To LAYTON*) It's for you, Inspector.

LAYTON: (*To TIM*) Thank you.

LAYTON takes the receiver from TIM.

LAYTON: Hello?

REED: This is Reed, sir. I'm rather worried about the Dorking situation.

LAYTON: (*Quickly*) What do you mean?

REED: There's no sign of life, sir – the office is in complete darkness.

LAYTON: (*Anxiously*) Do you think he's given you the slip?

REED: I don't see how he could have done, sir. We've been here since Forester left.

LAYTON: Has he had any visitors?

REED: Yes, several. A woman picked up a car at about half past six.

LAYTON: You're sure Dorking wasn't in the back of the car?

REED: No, I saw him return to the office.

LAYTON: Well, what's worrying you – perhaps he's cooking the books?

REED: With the light out, sir?

LAYTON: Have you got a hunch, Reed?

REED: Yes, sir. I don't like it.

LAYTON: (*Briskly*) Right! I'll be with you in fifteen minutes. We'll take a look.

CUT TO: DORKING's Office. Night.

We hear the sound of banging on the door. Suddenly the door is broken open from outside and REED and LAYTON burst open. They find DORKING lying on the floor.

LAYTON: (*To REED*) Phone for an ambulance and tell them we need a doctor.

REED picks up the telephone receiver and dials 999.

REED: (*On the phone*) Ambulance Service? This is Detective Sergeant Reed, Hammersmith Police. Will you send an ambulance and doctor to Dorking's Car Lot, Bridge Road.

DORKING: (*In pain*) Don't … Don't …

LAYTON: It's all right, Dorking. Don't worry, we'll soon have a doctor here …

DORKING: (*Deliriously*) Don't … bank … Colby …

LAYTON: (*Puzzled*) What is it? Did you say Colby?

DORKING: (*Still delirious*) Don't touch me, don't …

LAYTON: It's all right, Dorking. I'm here to help you …

DORKING: Don't … bank … Colby …

117

REED: What's he saying, sir?

LAYTON: (*Puzzled*) It sounds to me like – don't bank on Colby.

CUT TO: The Entrance Hall of TIM's Flat. Same Night.

TIM enters from the studio and opens the door. ALISON FORD is standing in the doorway.

TIM: (*Surprised*) Alison!

ALISON: Mr Forester, can I see you … for … a … moment?

TIM: Why, yes! Of course! Come in!

ALISON enters the hall and TIM closes the front door.

CUT TO: TIM's Studio Flat.

TIM and ALISON enter.

TIM: This is a surprise! I didn't know you were coming to Town or I'd have offered you a lift.

ALISON: (*Still breathless; unable to control herself*) Mr Forester, I'm sorry … to … disturb you like this, but … but …

TIM: Now wait a minute! Take it easy!

ALISON: I'll be all right when I get … my breath back. I … I rushed here because …

TIM: (*Amused*) Relax! Sit down. Take it easy.

ALISON sits.

TIM: Would you like a drink?

ALISON: Yes. Yes, I … I think I … would.

TIM: You think you would. Splendid. What would you like – whisky, gin?

ALISON: I don't mind.

TIM: Well, there's a little thing I did myself – it's most effective.

TIM mixes them both a drink. He hands a glass to ALISON.

TIM: Here we are. It's all right; it won't hurt you. It's known as a Petrified Forester.

ALISON sips her drink.

ALISON: It's delicious.

TIM: Good. (*A pause*) Now what's this all about?

ALISON: Mr Forester, did you telephone and ask …

TIM: (*Interrupting her*) I'm just a little tired of Mr Forester, Miss Briggs. Tim.

ALISON: All right – Tim. Did you phone at about half past six and ask me to meet you at a restaurant?

TIM: Phone? How could I? There isn't a phone at the caravan, is there?

ALISON: No, but there's a farm about half a mile away. If anyone wants to get in touch with Mary, they usually telephone the farm and leave a message. About half past six tonight the little girl came across and said that a Mr Forester had phoned and would Miss Hepburn's friend meet him at the Firenze Restaurant.

TIM: The Firenze Restaurant?

ALISON: Yes – at nine o'clock.

TIM: It wasn't me. I didn't phone you. Was that the complete message?

ALISON: The little girl said, the gentleman said it was urgent.

TIM: Do you know the Firenze Restaurant?

ALISON: No, I've never heard of it.

TIM: I'll look it up.

TIM goes to the table and looks the restaurant up in a directory.

TIM: (*Looking up*) It's in Orchard Street.

ALISON: Where's that?

TIM: Off the Edgware Road. (*He looks at his wristlet watch*) It's a quarter past nine. Whoever sent that message is probably still there, waiting for you. Look, Alison – I'm going to keep that

119

appointment. Will you wait here for me, I'll be back as soon as I can.

ALISON: Would you like me to come with you?

TIM: (*Thoughtfully*) No. No, I don't think that's a very good idea.

TIM goes out into the alcove and then returns putting on his coat. ALISON notices the photographs and picks one up.

ALISON: Are these the photographs my father brought?

TIM: Yes.

ALISON: And the dress?

TIM: Alison …

ALISON: Yes?

TIM: If anyone rings – don't answer the door. I've got my key. I shall let myself in.

ALISON: (*Puzzled*) Yes, all right. Tim, what happened this afternoon, after you left me?

TIM: I did what I told you I was going to do. I went straight to Scotland Yard.

ALISON: Did you see the Inspector?

TIM: Yes.

ALISON: Did you tell him about me?

TIM: (*Nodding*) Yes, I told him; but don't worry, I kept my promise. I didn't tell him who you are staying with.

ALISON: (*Quietly*) Thank you. I don't want to get Mary mixed up in this business; she's been an awfully good friend to me. I don't know what I should have done without her.

TIM: (*Facing ALISON*) But I did tell the Inspector you'd see him tomorrow afternoon.

ALISON: Where?

TIM: Here, at three o'clock.

ALISON: Yes, all right.

TIM: (*Quietly; looking at ALISON*) I shan't be long.
            Now remember what I told you. Don't answer the
            door.
ALISON: No.
TIM leaves.

CUT TO: A street in Soho, London.
We see the entrance to the Firenze Restaurant.

CUT TO: Inside the Firenze Restaurant.
Tim enters. A bottle of Chianti on a tray is being carried by a waiter blocking Tim's view of what is happening. As the waiter moves on, we see NORMAN BRIGGS sitting at a table.

END OF EPISODE FOUR

EPISODE FIVE

OPEN TO: Inside the Firenze Restaurant.

A bottle of Chianti is on BRIGGS's table. Tim's hand appears and closes round the neck of the bottle. He lifts the bottle off the table. TIM looks at the label on the bottle and then replaces it on the table. BRIGGS is staring up at TIM in astonishment.

TIM: Are you fond of Chianti, Mr Briggs?

BRIGGS: (*Rising*) Why, hello, Forester! This is a surprise! I've never seen you here before.

TIM: I've never been here before. Is this a favourite haunt of yours?

BRIGGS: (*Puzzled by TIM's attitude*) Yes, I suppose it is. I usually eat here two or three times a week when I'm in Town. The food's very good and the service is passable, if you're not too fussy. (*Smiles at TIM*) Have you had dinner?

TIM: (*Watching BRIGGS*) Yes.

BRIGGS: Are you alone?

TIM: Yes.

BRIGGS: Well, sit down – have some coffee with me.

TIM looks at BRIGGS for a moment, then sits down at the table. BRIGGS beckons a waiter who is out of the picture.

BRIGGS: Waiter!

TIM: Don't let me disturb your meal.

BRIGGS: No, no, I've finished, I've eaten far too much.

BRIGGS takes a cigar out of his breast pocket.

BRIGGS: I'm sorry I can't offer you a cigar.

TIM: (*Quietly*) That's all right.

BRIGGS examines the cigar; takes out a piercer.

BRIGGS: (*Smiling at TIM*) Well, this is a pleasant surprise. I wasn't expecting company.

TIM: Weren't you, Mr Briggs?

BRIGGS: No. Did you think I was?

TIM: The thought did occur to me.

BRIGGS: (*Faintly amused*) Whatever gave you that idea? Who did you think I was expecting – a lady friend?

BRIGGS puts the cigar in his mouth. There is a pause.

TIM: (*Almost completely matter of fact*) I thought perhaps you were expecting your daughter.

BRIGGS: (*Taking the cigar out of his mouth*) My daughter?

TIM: Yes.

BRIGGS: You mean – Alison? But Alison's dead! She was killed in that car accident with your brother. You know that as well as I do!

TIM: (*Shaking his head*) Alison's alive! Very much alive. I was with her less than half an hour ago.

BRIGGS: But that's impossible, man! I know for a fact that she ... (*He hesitates; stares at TIM*) Is this some kind of a practical joke? Because if it is it's in damn bad taste!

TIM: This isn't a joke, practical or otherwise. Your daughter's alive; she was asked to meet me here, tonight, in this restaurant.

BRIGGS: (*Puzzled*) To meet you?

TIM: Yes.

BRIGGS: (*Bewildered*) I don't understand this.

TIM: Someone sent Alison a message, saying that I wanted to see her. Instead of keeping the appointment she came to the Studio. That's why I'm here, Mr Briggs. I want to know who sent that message.

BRIGGS: You don't think I sent it?

TIM: Well, if you didn't, whoever did must have known that you were going to be here.

BRIGGS: (*Suddenly; tensely*) I don't believe all this! I don't believe Alison is alive!

126

TIM: (*Quietly*) Briggs, if Alison isn't alive, why should I say that she is?

BRIGGS stares at TIM; he looks puzzled; almost dejected.

BRIGGS: Forester, is this the truth – really the truth – about Alison?

TIM: Yes.

BRIGGS: But have you known all along – did you know she was alive the day I brought the photographs?

TIM: No.

BRIGGS: Well, when did you find out? When did you first see Alison?

TIM: This afternoon.

BRIGGS: Where – in London?

TIM: No, I went down to … (*Changes his mind*) … where she was staying.

BRIGGS: But why is she hiding like this? Why hasn't she got in touch with me? I don't understand it, surely her own father … (*He stops; looks at TIM*) Did she mention me at all?

TIM: Yes.

BRIGGS: Well – what did she say?

TIM: (*A moment*) She said a number of things, some of them not entirely complimentary.

BRIGGS: What do you mean?

TIM: She said you introduced her to my brother because you suspected that he was making certain inquiries …

BRIGGS: Inquiries?

TIM: About you and your business.

BRIGGS: Then why should I introduce my daughter to him?

TIM: You wanted her to find out exactly what Lewis was up to.

BRIGGS: (*Shocked*) Did Alison tell you that?

TIM: She did.

BRIGGS: But this is fantastic, I can hardly believe she'd do such a thing. (*He looks at TIM; quietly*) Yet you believe her, don't you, Forester?

TIM: Wouldn't you believe her, if you were in my shoes?

BRIGGS: (*Almost a sigh of resignation*) Yes, I suppose I would.

BRIGGS puts his cigar down on the table.

BRIGGS: You know, life's funny. You can spend years looking after a person, being devoted to them, spending hard earned money on them, and then suddenly – when you need them more than anything else in the world – they let you down.

TIM: Do you consider Alison has let you down?

BRIGGS looks at TIM; there is a long pause.

BRIGGS: No, no, I must be fair. I've always known Alison's limitations; to me, at any rate, she's never pretended to be anything other than what she is.

TIM: What do you mean by that?

BRIGGS: (*With his hand on the Chianti bottle*) You don't know my daughter very well, do you, Mr Forester?

TIM: I don't know you very well, Mr Briggs.

BRIGGS hesitates, then picks up the bottle of wine. He pours Tim a glass of wine and then turns towards his own glass and tops it up.

BRIGGS: Before we go any further, I think perhaps I'd better tell you one or two things about Alison …

CUT TO: TIM's Studio Flat.

ALISON is at the centre table pouring coffee for herself and TIM. She adds milk to one of the cups, picks it up, and offers it to TIM. TIM looks thoughtful and serious.

ALISON: I hope you didn't mind my making coffee while you were away?

TIM takes the coffee cup.

TIM: It was an excellent idea; I'm glad you thought of it.

ALISON: (*Sipping her coffee; then looking up at TIM*) Well – you still haven't told me what happened. Was there anyone at the restaurant?

TIM: Yes.

ALISON: Anyone I know?

TIM: Yes, Alison – someone we both know.

ALISON: Someone we both … (*Suddenly*) My father!

TIM: (*Quietly*) Yes.

ALISON: Was it my father who sent the message asking me to meet you?

TIM: (*Shaking his head*) He says not.

ALISON: But it must have been, otherwise what was he doing at the restaurant?

TIM: The message could have been sent by someone else; someone who knew that your father was going to be there.

ALISON: (*Faintly irritated*) Is that the explanation he gave you?

TIM: (*Sips his coffee; after a moment*) Yes. Yes, it is.

ALISON: And you believe it?

TIM: (*Still watching ALISON; slowly*) I think it's a possible explanation – yes.

ALISON: So, whoever sent the message must have known that my father was going to be at that particular restaurant at that particular time?

TIM: Yes, but that isn't quite so far fetched as it sounds. In the first place, your father has a habit of dining there and in the second place more often

129

than not he reserves a table. He reserved one tonight.

ALISON: Well?

TIM: Well, anyone could have phoned the restaurant and found out if he was going to be there.

ALISON: (*Shaking her head*) My father sent that message, I'm sure of it. He knew I'd seen you and he tried to trick me into meeting him.

TIM: (*Quietly*) Alison, why won't you meet your father?

ALISON: (*Tensely*) Because I never want to see him again – never!

TIM: He doesn't feel that way about you; he's prepared to let the past …

ALISON: (*Putting down her coffee cup on the table*) Listen, Tim, there's lots of things I don't know about my father, but I know him a great deal better than you do. Don't be taken in by him.

TIM: (*Quietly*) I'm not taken in by him, Alison.

ALISON: I think you are. What was he like tonight? Friendly … a shade sentimental … just a little hurt when my name was mentioned?

TIM: Yes, I think that best describes his mood.

ALISON: (*Nodding; a shade angry*) Did he tell you about my mother, and what happened the day she died? Did he tell you about the first school I went to and how disappointed he was when he found that I was, well – not exactly a liar, but …

TIM: (*Faintly surprised by ALISON's frankness*) Yes. Yes, he did.

ALISON: What else did he tell you, Mr Forester?

TIM: He said he had to take you abroad because you were having an affair with a married man.

ALISON: Go on …

TIM: He said that no sooner were you over that affair
            than you were running after someone else.
ALISON: Go on …
TIM: He said that time and time again, he'd had
            trouble with you because …
ALISON: Because I was impetuous, impressionable, and
            incurably romantic.
TIM: Yes, those were his exact words.
ALISON: I gather he didn't actually call me a
            nymphomaniac?
TIM: Er – no.
ALISON: But he left you with the impression that he might
            have done, except for the fact that – well, after all,
            I am his daughter, and he's a jolly nice chap.
TIM: (*Thoughtfully*) Yes. Yes, I suppose that's true.
ALISON: (*Softly*) Go on …
TIM: He denied your story about Lewis: he said he'd
            never even heard of him until – you picked him
            up in Milan …
ALISON: (*Unable to conceal her anger*) That's not true!
TIM: (*Facing Alison*) He said you refused to go to
            Sicily simply because you wanted to stay with
            Lewis. There was no question of your finding out
            anything.
ALISON: My father asked me to stay behind, he
            deliberately encouraged me to get friendly with
            your brother.
TIM: Why?
ALISON: (*Angrily*) I've told you why! He wanted me to find
            out certain things!
TIM: Yes, but what things!?
ALISON: (*After a pause; hesitant*) He wanted to know what
            your brother was doing in Italy; he wanted a
            report from me on the people he met; he asked

131

me to find out why Lewis telephoned a man in Rome, called Greneko.

TIM: (*Apparently not convinced*) But why should your father want to know those things if he'd never even heard of Lewis?

ALISON: Of course he'd heard of him! The day we arrived at Milan he inquired if your brother had registered at the hotel; that was the very first thing he asked.

TIM: Are you sure of that?

ALISON: Of course I'm sure. I asked him who Lewis Forester was.

TIM: And what did he say?

ALISON: He said he was just a man he was hoping to do business with. Later, when Lewis arrived, he went out of his way to get an introduction to him.

TIM: (*Quietly; puzzled*) I see.

TIM drinks his coffee; he looks thoughtful, perplexed.

ALISON: (*Quietly*) Tim …

TIM: (*Looking up*) Yes?

ALISON: Did you tell my father where I was staying?

TIM: No; but if he sent that message, then obviously he knows.

ALISON: (*A suggestion of a smile*) He didn't ask you?

TIM: (*Thoughtfully*) No, as a matter of fact, he didn't. (*He looks up*) He said he wanted to see you and I told him to telephone me tomorrow morning.

ALISON: (*Determined*) I'm not seeing him.

TIM: (*A moment; then*) All right, Alison. That's up to you.

There is a pause. ALISON watches TIM for a moment; he is sipping his coffee, deep in thought.

ALISON: It's a problem, isn't it?

TIM: Yes, Alison, it's a problem.

ALISON: (*Slowly; with almost a strange note of sympathy in her voice*) You just don't know who to believe.

TIM looks at ALISON over his coffee cup.

CUT TO: *A stream-lined Daimler, LCC, Ambulance is racing through the London streets: the Accident sign flashing on and off. The ambulance bell is ringing.*

CUT TO: A bed in the Accident Ward of a London Hospital. There is a chair by the side of the bed, and a bedside table with cupboard. On top of the table are a packet of cigarettes, a cheque book, a wristlet watch, and a cigarette lighter.

REG DORKING is the patient in bed. He is swathed in bandages and there are several pieces of sticking plaster on his face and hands. He is smoking a cigarette. An attractive young NURSE appears; she takes the cigarette out of his mouth and puts in a thermometer. DORKING immediately removes the thermometer and returns it to the NURSE.

DORKING: It's ninety-eight point four …
NURSE: How do you know?
DORKING: That's normal, isn't it?
NURSE: Yes.
DORKING: Well, I'm normal – (*Looking at the NURSE*) in every respect.
NURSE: Mr Dorking, I've got to take your temperature so will you please …
DORKING: Now listen, sister …
NURSE: I'm not a Sister!
DORKING: (*Moving; and wincing with paid*) Okay, you're not a sister – you're a Grandmother. Now get the hell out of here, that's a good kid.

DETECTIVE INSPECTOR LAYTON arrives; he looks at the
NURSE and nods. The NURSE leaves. DORKING stares at
LAYTON; he tries to make himself comfortable.

DORKING: Hello! What are you doing here?

LAYTON: Do you feel any better?

DORKING: I feel terrific. No bones broken – just crushed.

LAYTON sits on the chair by the side of the bed.

LAYTON: I want to have a little chat, Dorking.

DORKING: Fine, dear boy! I'm just in the mood for light
            conversation.

LAYTON: (*Indicating DORKING's bandages*) Who did
            this? Who beat you up?

DORKING: Gilbert Harding.

LAYTON: Now listen, Dorking, if you've got any sense
            in that head of yours ...

DORKING: Right now, I've got sixteen sledgehammers
            and four pneumatic drills.

LAYTON: Yes, I expect you feel pretty rotten but ...

DORKING: You can say that again!

LAYTON: ... but I've got to talk to you. (*Quietly*) Now
            who did this? Was it the man who gave you
            the card?

DORKING: Which card?

LAYTON: (*Quite friendly; leaning forward*) Dorking, we
            know all about David Forester. We know all
            about ...

DORKING: (*Holding his head*) Okay, dear boy, you know
            all about everything – that's fine! Now leave
            me alone ... (*Turns and looks away: calling*)
            Sister! I want a Scotch and ... (*Winces*) ...
            soda ...

LAYTON: (*Quietly*) You know, I just don't think you
            realise just how serious this situation is.

DORKING: Are you kiddin'?

LAYTON:	Someone gave you that card and told you to flog it for them; now we want to know …
DORKING:	'Flog' it, that's a nice word for a Detective-Inspector.
LAYTON:	We want to know who that person was, Dorking.
DORKING:	(*Irritated*) Listen, I don't know what you're talking about. I don't know anything about a card. Now do me a favour – beat it!
LAYTON:	When we picked you up tonight, you mentioned the name Colby.
DORKING:	Did I?
LAYTON:	Yes.
DORKING:	I don't remember.
LAYTON:	You said something that sounded like … Don't bank on Colby … or bank <u>and</u> Colby … or something like that.
DORKING:	(*Quietly; shaking his head*) I don't remember.
LAYTON:	You remember all right. (*Leaning forward; confidentially*) You thought you'd had it and you were trying to say something. Now come on, what was it, there's a good chap.
DORKING:	(*A shade angry*) I've told you. I don't remember!
LAYTON:	Now, Dorking, listen – whoever beat you up tonight will probably …
DORKING:	Beat me up! What do you mean – beat me up? I had an accident. A cupboard fell on top of me.
LAYTON:	(*Rising; faintly exasperated*) Are you sure it wasn't your overheads?

LAYTON moves the chair; and turns away from the bed.

DORKING:	(*Quietly*) Inspector …
LAYTON:	(*Turning*) Yes?

DORKING: (*Grinning*) Next time you come, bring some
                     grapes.

*LAYTON looks at DORKING for a moment and then turns
away again, as he does so he quite deliberately knocks the
cheque book off the table.*

LAYTON: (*Excessively polite*) Oh, I beg your pardon.

*LAYTON stoops and picks up the cheque book. He flicks
through the cheque book, glancing at the cheques. He returns
the book to the table.*

LAYTON: Sorry about that. (*He smiles and nods to
                     DORKING*) I'll try and remember the grapes.

*DORKING looks puzzled. He picks up the cheque book; looks
at it; then looks after the INSPECTOR as he leaves.*

CUT TO: TIM's Studio Flat. Night.

*The studio is in darkness; but there is the sound of the
doorbell ringing. TIM enters from the bedroom – wearing a
dressing gown – he switches on the lights and crosses to the
alcove.*

CUT TO: The Entrance Hall of TIM's flat.

*TIM enters from the studio and opens the front door. HENRY
CARMICHAEL is standing in the doorway. He looks faintly
worried.*

HENRY: Hello, Forester! I hope I haven't got you out
                     of bed?

TIM: No, that's all right. Come in!

HENRY enters and Tim closes the door.

HENRY: I didn't know whether to come straight back
                     or not. I nearly telephoned you, but I thought
                     perhaps the Inspector might still be here.

TIM: No, he left soon after you did.

CUT TO: TIM's Studio Flat.

HENRY enters, followed by TIM.

TIM: Did you drop Colby?

HENRY: Yes. (*He looks at TIM*) He's a curious man, isn't he?

TIM: Yes, I suppose he is. (*Facing HENRY*) Now what's all this about Mary Hepburn?

HENRY: (*Anxiously*) You didn't tell the police about Miss Hepburn, did you?

TIM: No, I told you. I haven't mentioned her.

HENRY takes out his handkerchief and mops his forehead.

HENRY: Good! I made a dreadful mistake, Forester. By George, I should have looked a damn fool if you'd gone to the police with that story of mine.

TIM: Look, Carmichael – let's get this straight. Did Mary Hepburn threaten Jill or didn't she?

HENRY: No, she didn't.

TIM: Then what was the point of your story?

HENRY: What do you mean?

TIM: You told me that Jill and Miss Hepburn were very good friends, then apparently, they had a row and Mary Hepburn threatened to murder her.

HENRY: Yes, I know I told you that, but I've just explained to you, I – I was mistaken.

TIM: Mistaken? You couldn't be mistaken about a thing like that!

HENRY: Yes, I was, Forester. You see, it's over six months ago and I was confusing Mary Hepburn with someone else.

TIM: You mean it was someone else who threatened to murder Jill?

HENRY: Yes.

TIM: Well – who was it?

HENRY: (*Shaking his head*) It's not important.

137

TIM: (*Annoyed*) What do you mean, it's not important? Of course it's important!

HENRY: No, no, you don't understand. It's not important simply because the person who threatened Jill is dead; she died before Jill was murdered.

TIM: (*Quietly; watching HENRY*) I see.

HENRY: I'm sorry, Forester, I know you thought Mary Hepburn was another suspect and obviously from your point of view …

TIM: (*Interrupting him*) Who was this other person?

HENRY: (*Surprised at being interrupted*) I beg your pardon?

TIM: I said: who was this other person?

A slight pause.

HENRY: There's no point in telling you because she's not a suspect – she can't be – she's dead.

TIM: Nevertheless, I'd like to know.

HENRY: Well, as a matter of fact – (*He points to a photograph of ALISON*) – it was Alison Ford.

TIM: (*Quietly; surprised*) Alison Ford?

HENRY: Yes.

TIM: But how do you know Alison even knew Jill?

HENRY: Of course she knew Jill! Alison Ford was a friend of Miss Hepburn's – so was Jill.

TIM: And it was Alison that had the row with Jill?

HENRY: Yes.

TIM: Well, what made you think it was Mary Hepburn?

HENRY: I've told you: I got confused. I knew the three of them were very friendly and I thought it was Jill and Mary Hepburn that had the row.

TIM: (*Quietly; watching HENRY*) Instead of which it was Jill and Alison Ford?

HENRY: Yes. (*Facing TIM*) You don't believe me, do you, Forester?

TIM: What was the row about, do you know?

HENRY: Yes.

TIM: Well?

HENRY: Look, Forester, there's no point in my telling you
         what the row was about, because Alison's dead.
         If she were alive then …

TIM: What was the row about?

HENRY looks at Tim, hesitates, then:

HENRY: Well, apparently Alison was friendly with some
         actor or other, and she accused Jill of trying to –
         what's the technical term? – alienate his
         affections.

TIM: (*Quietly*) I see.

HENRY: There was no truth in it, of course, but I gather –
         from what I've heard from other sources – that
         Alison was rather like that.

TIM: You mean …

HENRY: She was always having an affair with someone,
         and getting jealous and having rows, and – well,
         you know the sort of thing. (*He shakes his head*) I
         just don't know how people have time for all that
         nonsense.

TIM: Did you ever meet Alison?

HENRY: No; I didn't.

TIM: Or her father?

HENRY: No. There's no point in telling the police about all
         this. If Alison was alive, of course, that would be
         a very different story …

HENRY looks at TIM. A pause. He glances at his watch.

HENRY: Well, I suppose I'd better be making a move. (*A
         sudden thought*) Oh, do you think I could make a
         telephone call?

TIM appears to be deep in thought.

TIM: (*Looking up*) M'm?

139

HENRY: (*Smiling*) I said: do you think I could make a phone call?

TIM: Oh, yes, of course. I'm sorry. Is it private?

HENRY: No, no …

TIM: Well, use the extension, anyway. It's in the bedroom.

HENRY: Thank you.

HENRY turns and goes into the bedroom. TIM watches him, then thoughtfully turns and picks up a cigarette off the table. He lights the cigarette, looks towards the bedroom, and then crosses to a photograph of ALISON. He stands deep in thought, smoking, facing the photograph.

CUT TO: MAJOR COLBY's Office. Morning.

COLBY is sitting at the desk writing a letter. The door opens and INSPECTOR LAYTON enters. COLBY looks up and puts down his pen.

COLBY: Layton, what time is that appointment with Forester?

LAYTON: Three o'clock.

COLBY: Oh, good. I thought it was four, and I've a meeting at half-past.

LAYTON sits on the arm of a chair.

LAYTON: Do you think he'll produce the Briggs girl?

COLBY: He'd better, after what he told us last night.

LAYTON: I don't know why, but – I'm still dubious about Tim Forester.

COLBY: You don't think he did see Alison?

LAYTON: M'm – we'll see what happens this afternoon.

COLBY rises and comes round the front of the desk.

COLBY: Well – what's the news about Fenby?

LAYTON: There isn't any. He hasn't been to the office, no one's seen him, and he wasn't at his flat last night.

COLBY: (*Shaking his head*) I don't like it. You'd better get a description out and warn the transport people …

LAYTON: I've already done that.

LAYTON takes his pipe out of his pocket.

LAYTON: Major, you remember I told you that Dorking mentioned your name the other night?

MAJOR: Yes. You said he said something about Colby and the bank or something.

LAYTON: (*Nodding*) Yes. Well, I now know what he was getting at.

COLBY: What was he getting at?

LAYTON: He was trying to tell me that he'd written you a letter and that he'd deposited it with his bank manager.

COLBY: With his bank manager?

LAYTON: Yes.

LAYTON takes out his pouch and fills his pipe.

LAYTON: Last night, when I visited Dorking, I made a point of finding out the name of his bank. This morning I made a point of seeing his bank manager.

COLBY: (*Curious*) Go on.

LAYTON: Apparently two or three days ago Dorking handed Carter – that's the bank manager – a letter. The letter was addressed to you, it has your private address on it. He told Carter that under certain exceptional circumstances the letter was to be handed to you, personally.

COLBY: What did he mean – exceptional circumstances?

LAYTON: He meant if he was murdered – or attacked in any way.

COLBY: But he was attacked.

LAYTON lights his pipe; he looks at COLBY over the smoke.

LAYTON: Exactly.

141

LAYTON flicks out the match.

LAYTON: Carter's downstairs, in my office. He's got the letter.

COLBY stares at LAYTON, then smiles. COLBY goes out. LAYTON sits smoking, rather pleased with himself.

CUT TO: TIM's Studio Flat. Afternoon.

COLBY is standing near the dais, looking towards ALISON. TIM is standing near the easel; the INSPECTOR is sitting on the arm of the wing chair looking towards COLBY. There is a definite suggestion of tenseness.

ALISON: (*Exasperated*) … I've told you the truth, Major Colby. I remember the card. I remember it very well. It had a drawing on it. A bottle of Chianti and a girl's hand.

COLBY: But why should you remember that particular card?

ALISON: Because I was with Lewis the day he posted it.

COLBY: And you say it was posted in Naples?

ALISON: Yes, I've told you! It was posted in Naples and sent to a man called Peter Fenby.

COLBY: You're quite sure of the name – Fenby?

ALISON: Yes, of course I'm sure!

COLBY: (*With a non-committal nod*) Thank you, Miss Briggs.

COLBY moves towards the INSPECTOR.

ALISON: (*A shade indignant*) Well – do you believe me?

COLBY: (*Smiling*) A moment ago you told me it was a matter of complete indifference to you whether I believed you or not.

ALISON: (*Almost losing her temper*) Never mind what I said a moment ago! Do you believe me?

COLBY: (*After a pause*) Yes, I do.

ALISON: Well, that's something!

142

TIM: Congratulations, Alison! It isn't everyone that
           Major Colby believes.

LAYTON: (*To TIM*) In this particular instance, Miss Briggs
           was confirming what we already suspected, sir.

TIM: In short, she's told you what I told you yesterday
           afternoon – that Fenby's got the card.

LAYTON: Yes.

COLBY: Or had the card, Mr Forester – as the case may
           be.

TIM: Well, whether he's got it or had it, or never had it,
           don't you think it would be an excellent idea to
           ask Mr Fenby a few of these questions instead of
           Miss Briggs?

COLBY: I do indeed. Can you produce Mr Fenby for us?

TIM looks at COLBY, then at the INSPECTOR.

TIM: You mean …?

LAYTON: We're still trying to locate him, so far, we've
           drawn a blank.

TIM: I see.

COLBY: Miss Briggs …

ALISON: Miss Ford, please Major, or Alison, not Miss
           Briggs …

COLBY: Miss Ford, you said just now that your father
           encouraged you to get friendly with Lewis; that
           he asked you to make certain enquiries.

ALISON: Yes.

COLBY: What were those enquiries?

ALISON: He wanted to know what Lewis was doing in
           Milan and why he telephoned a man in Rome
           called Greneko.

COLBY: Anything else?

ALISON: Yes – he asked me to find out if Lewis was a
           friend of … (*She hesitates*)

COLBY: Go on …

ALISON: (*After a pause*) He asked me to find out if Lewis was a friend of yours, Major Colby.

COLBY: And did you?

ALISON: (*Shaking her head*) Lewis never mentioned you; not to me, at any rate.

LAYTON: Miss Ford, did your father mention the card at all?

ALISON: No.

LAYTON: So, in actual fact, when you saw the card you didn't think it was at all important?

ALISON: No, I didn't.

TIM: (*Quietly*) Major Colby …

COLBY: Yes?

TIM: Who's this man Greneko?

COLBY looks across at LAYTON.

LAYTON: He's an Italian newspaper correspondent: a crime reporter.

TIM: Was he a friend of my brother's?

LAYTON: I should imagine so.

ALISON: (*Puzzled*) Well, why was my father interested in him?

LAYTON: (*Watching ALISON*) Was he interested in him, Miss Ford?

ALISON: He must have been. He wanted to know about the phone call.

COLBY: About a year ago, Greneko wrote an article for an Italian magazine. The article was re-published in one of the digests and created quite a stir.

LAYTON: (*To TIM*) It's my bet that's when your brother first met Greneko.

TIM: But what was the article about?

COLBY: (*After a pause*) About the Arlington Ring …

TIM: The Arlington Ring?

ALISON: What's that?

144

COLBY: It's the name given to a group of people. There was at one time a man called Arlington – Ross Arlington – but he died about two years ago. Since then, the group has been controlled, or organised if you like, by – someone else.

TIM: But what is this group? Is it a political organisation?

LAYTON: No.

COLBY: (*Smiling*) They're not interested in politics, Mr Forester.

TIM: Well, what are they interested in?

There is a tiny pause. TIM looks at the INSPECTOR and then across at COLBY.

COLBY: Diamonds.

TIM: Diamonds?

COLBY: (*Nodding*) Yes.

ALISON: (*Hesitant; to the INSPECTOR*) Do you mean that this group – the Arlington Ring, as you call them – have been smuggling diamonds?

LAYTON: Yes.

ALISON: But from where – not from Italy, surely?

LAYTON: From South Africa.

COLBY: The stones were smuggled into Italy, brought over here by one of the Arlington Ring and then taken to New York.

TIM: Yes, but just how serious is this business?

COLBY: Very serious. The Diamond Corporation of South Africa are desperate; they've contacted every police organisation in Europe – not to mention the F.B.I.

TIM: But is the supply of diamonds controlled?

COLBY: The legitimate supply yes – very carefully controlled. That is the whole point. The

145

Arlington Ring have broken through the control and are affecting the world market.

ALISON: Major Colby …

COLBY: Yes?

ALISON: You said just now that the head of the group used to be a man called Arlington …

COLBY: (*Nodding*) That's right, but Arlington's dead. His place has been taken by someone else.

There is a pause. COLBY looks at TIM as does ALISON.

ALISON: Who is the – someone else? Do you know?

COLBY: We're not sure. But your brother knew, Mr Forester.

CUT TO: *A car drives up to a telephone box in a deserted country lane. PETER FENBY gets out of the car and enters the box. We see him dialling a number.*

CUT TO: TIM's Studio Flat.

The telephone is ringing. TIM lifts the receiver. For the duration of this conversation, we cut back and forth between TIM and FENBY in the phone box.

TIM: (*On the phone*) Hello?

FENBY: (*On the other end of the phone*) Is that Tim Forester?

TIM: Yes.

FENBY: This is Peter Fenby.

TIM: (*Quickly; tensely*) Fenby, where are you? Where are you speaking from?

FENBY: (*Smiling*) I'm in a call box.

TIM: Yes, but where?

FENBY: Oh, tucked away, old boy. Back of beyond.

TIM: Fenby, listen – we've been trying to get in touch with you.

FENBY: Have you, old chap?

TIM:	Inspector Layton wants to see you. It's urgent, Fenby. Go straight to Scotland Yard.
FENBY:	I'm afraid under the circumstances that's not a very bright suggestion.
TIM:	What do you mean?
FENBY:	(*Seriously*) Forester, listen – I've posted something to you. It's very important, you'll get it first post tomorrow morning.
TIM:	(*Puzzled*) Well – what is it?
FENBY:	You'll recognise it when you see it. Please yourself what you do with it, Forester. It's your responsibility from now on.

FENBY replaces the receiver.

TIM:	Hello? … Fenby … Fenby …

TIM rattles the receiver.

CUT TO: *FENBY leaves the telephone box and returns to his car. He gets into the car and drives off.*

CUT TO: *FENBY drives his car onto a private drive of an Aero Club. There is an aircraft on the runway. The car comes to a standstill; FENBY gets out of the car and lifts a small case from the back seat. He looks up, towards a shed on the edge of the drive. A man, wearing flying kit, comes out of the shed. He is CHARLES WHITE. WHITE notices FENBY and waves a greeting. FENBY waves back and starts walking towards CHARLES. CHARLES waits for FENBY by the hut. FENBY arrives.*

FENBY:	(*Pleasantly*) Hello, Charles, old boy. You look disgustingly well, as usual.
CHARLES:	(*A shade worried*) Pete, what's this all about?
FENBY:	I told you, I'm chasing a big story. It's red hot. I've got to be in Paris by seven o'clock.
CHARLES:	Paris? I can't fly you to Paris!

FENBY: No-one's asking you to. Now stop worrying!
            All you've got to do is dump me on the other
            side.
CHARLES: (*Shaking his head*) I don't like this sort of
            lark! It's dicey.
FENBY: Nonsense!
CHARLES: (*Pointing*) What's in that case?
FENBY: Pound notes.
CHARLES: Ha – ha – very funny! All right, let's get
            cracking!

CUT TO: The front door of Tim's flat.
*DAVID FORRESTER is standing at the door pressing the
bell. He is dressed in a lounge suit and carries his hat. After
a moment, the door is opened by TIM who is obviously
surprised to see DAVID. TIM wears a dressing-gown, and his
hair is faintly dishevelled.*
TIM: (*Surprised*) Oh, hello, David! I thought it was
            the post.
DAVID: Good morning, Tim! Have I got you out of
            the bath?
TIM: Good heavens no! I've been up hours.
            (*Smiling*) At least five minutes!
DAVID laughs and enters the flat.

CUT TO: TIM's Studio flat.
TIM enters followed by DAVID.
TIM: Have you had breakfast?
DAVID: Yes – ages ago.
TIM: Well, let me get you some coffee.
DAVID: No, no, don't bother, Tim, unless you
            particularly want some.

TIM:	No, I've had breakfast. (*Facing DAVID*) Well, what brings you to Town at the crack of dawn?
DAVID:	(*Smiling*) Half-past eight – the crack of dawn?
TIM:	It must have been considerably earlier when you left St Albans.
DAVID:	Yes, as a matter of fact it was seven o'clock.
TIM:	David, you seem to be having rather a lot of appointments in London just lately.
DAVID:	Yes, I do, don't I? It's making you quite curious, isn't it, Tim?
TIM:	What do you mean?
DAVID:	You followed me to Dorking's the other afternoon.
TIM:	(*Faintly embarrassed*) Yes, I know. I'm sorry about that.
DAVID:	Did Colby explain?
TIM:	Yes.
DAVID:	I'm glad. It was rather difficult for me; I just didn't quite know what to say to you.
TIM:	(*Watching DAVID*) You lied like an expert, David.
DAVID:	(*Smiling*) Thank you, Tim.
TIM:	I take it your appointment isn't with Dorking this morning?
DAVID:	No, it isn't. It's with a gentleman called Sir Harold Maze.
TIM:	Sir Harold Maze?
DAVID:	Yes. He's the Chairman and Managing Director and what-have-you of Spencer and Maze.
TIM:	Spencer and Maze? Aren't they the publishers?

DAVID: Yes. They publish textbooks. Very heavy books at
           very heavy prices.

TIM: Well, why should he want to see you?

DAVID: He's offered me a job, Tim.

TIM: (*Puzzled*) A job?

DAVID: Yes. They're opening an office in Melbourne and
           he's offered me the job of general manager.

TIM: But you don't know anything about publishing!

DAVID: No, but I have read some of their books. Believe
           me, that's a unique qualification.

TIM: David, are you serious about this?

DAVID: Perfectly.

TIM: Do you want to live in Australia?

DAVID: I've never really considered that aspect of it; I
           certainly don't want to go on living at St Albans.

TIM: This is extraordinary. I thought … (*He stops
           speaking; suddenly*) Excuse me.

*TIM crosses to the alcove; DAVID watches him with obvious
curiosity. After a moment, TIM returns.*

TIM: I'm sorry, David. I thought it was the post.

DAVID: (*Amused*) There was quite a glint in your eye
           when you answered the door. Have you won a
           football pool or something?

TIM: No such luck. David, are you going to accept this
           offer?

DAVID: I think so, yes. It's six hundred a year more than
           I'm getting at the moment; that's not to be
           sneezed at.

TIM: But I thought you liked teaching? You always
           wanted to be a teacher.

DAVID: I'm bored with it, Tim. Besides, an extra six
           hundred a year, old boy.

TIM: (*Facing DAVID; a shade puzzled*) But you always
           used to say that money was unimportant. My

150

	God, the time you lectured me – and Lewis – about it.
DAVID:	That was before I had any.
TIM:	(*Curious*) Have you got some now, then?
DAVID:	(*With a nervous little laugh*) No, I didn't mean that. I …
TIM:	What did you mean?
DAVID:	Look, Tim, it seems to me that the most important thing in life is to do what you want to do.
TIM:	Exactly.
DAVID:	Well, I want to go to Australia.
TIM:	But you haven't always wanted to go to Australia.
DAVID:	People change.

DAVID turns and walks round the studio; TIM watches him. DAVID stands for a moment looking at a sketch of TIM's.

DAVID:	That's rather pleasant, Tim – is it new?
TIM:	(*Quietly; serious*) David …
DAVID:	(*Turning*) Yes?
TIM:	Supposing this job was in America, or New Zealand, or South Africa even …
DAVID:	Well?
TIM:	Well, would you still take it?
DAVID:	Yes.
TIM:	In other words, you just want to get out of the country.

DAVID crosses to TIM.

DAVID:	Tim, I want a change; a complete change. At the moment I'm in a vacuum, an intellectual deep-freeze. If I stay in this country, I know exactly what will happen to me. Five years from now I shall be a crashing bore; in ten years a dehydrated Mr Chips.

TIM: (*A moment; a suggestion of a sigh*) All right,
           David. I suppose you know what's best for you.
DAVID: (*Smiling*) I wouldn't say that, Tim. But I know
           what I'm going to do.
TIM suddenly looks towards the alcove.

CUT TO: The Entrance Hall of TIM's flat.
*Several letters are in the process of being pushed through the
letterbox; they drop on the floor. TIM enters from the studio.
He stoops down and picks up the letters. He stands sorting
them out; finally giving his attention to one particular
envelope. He looks at the envelope – at the postmark. After a
moment he opens it and takes out a postcard. His expression
changes.*

CUT TO: Tim's Studio Flat.
*TIM quickly enters from the alcove and crosses to the
telephone.*
TIM: (*To DAVID*) Excuse me, David, I've got to make a
           phone call.
TIM lifts the telephone receiver and starts dialling.
DAVID: (*Quietly*) Put the phone down, Tim – there's a
           good chap.
*TIM looks up, towards DAVID. His expression is very serious.
He slowly replaces the receiver. DAVID is now facing Tim
with a revolver in his hand.*
DAVID: (*Quite pleasantly; yet serious*) I want that card,
           Tim.

END OF EPISODE FIVE

EPISODE SIX

OPEN TO: TIM's Studio Flat.

TIM lifts the telephone receiver and starts dialling.

DAVID: (*Quietly*) Put the phone down, Tim – there's a good chap.

TIM looks up, towards DAVID. His expression is very serious. He slowly replaces the receiver. DAVID is now facing Tim with a revolver in his hand.

DAVID: (*Quite pleasantly; yet serious*) I want that card, Tim.

TIM: (*Quietly, moving towards DAVID*) David, are you serious?

DAVID: (*Holding out his hand*) Give me that card …

TIM: (*Suddenly; amused*) This is a joke! That thing's not loaded, you're just …

DAVID: (*Interrupting him; a shade angry*) Tim, I want that card!

TIM's expression changes; he looks at DAVID. There is a pause. TIM looks at DAVID. There is a pause. DAVID moves towards TIM.

DAVID: Give it to me!

TIM: (*Shaking his head*) I'm not going to give it to you, David.

DAVID: I warn you, Tim, if you don't … (*He raises the revolver*) This isn't a toy. I shall use it …

TIM faces David. A slight pause.

TIM: All right. Go ahead, use it …

DAVID: (*A shade angry; a serious threat*) I'm going to give you five seconds, Tim.

TIM: (*Suddenly angry*) I don't care whether you give me five seconds, or five minutes, or five hours! If you're going to use that thing, use it!

There is a long pause, then TIM turns and sits on the arm of a chair. He points to the revolver.

TIM: That makes no difference. You might just as well throw it out of the window.

DAVID: (*Softly; yet with a note of desperation*) Tim, I'm desperate, I've got to have that card. If you don't give it to me I … I really will kill you …

TIM: (*Shaking his head*) No, David. You've either got to be very stupid to use one of those, or very brave. I don't think you're either.

DAVID: (*Tensely; determined*) All right. Walk over to that telephone and ring Major Colby, tell him you've got the card.

TIM: (*Quietly; a shade worried*) And what happens if I do that?

DAVID: I shall convince you that I'm either very brave, or very stupid.

There is a pause, then TIM rises and, turning his back on DAVID, walks slowly over to the table and telephone and as he reaches the table however he hesitates and turns.

TIM: (*Suddenly*) David, what's so important about this card?

DAVID: Unless I'm mistaken, it's got my name on it.

TIM looks at DAVID, then down at the card he is holding.

TIM: (*Moving towards David again*) No, it's got nothing on it, except Fenby's name and address – and the drawing of course. You can see for yourself.

TIM holds the card out towards DAVID and without thinking his brother stretches out his hand. Immediately he does so, TIM drops the card and springs into action in an attempt to try and knock the revolver out of DAVID's hand. Although taken unawares, DAVID quickly realises what is happening and refuses to drop the revolver. TIM grips DAVID's arm and a struggle ensues for the possession of the revolver. Suddenly, there is a shot and DAVID drops the revolver and staggers back from TIM holding his chest. TIM stands horrified, staring at his brother. There is a long pause then DAVID, still clutching his chest, moves across towards the wing chair.

TIM:　　　(*Softly; staggered*) David! David …

DAVID sinks into the chair. TIM crosses to DAVID.

DAVID:　　(*Mechanically; not looking at TIM*) Where's – where's the card?

TIM looks round, then notices the card on the floor near the chair and picks it up.

TIM:　　　(*Quietly*) It's here …

DAVID:　　(*In obvious pain; gasping slightly*) Destroy it, Tim … Don't let the police get it …

DAVID clutches his chest and falls forward.

DAVID:　　Don't …

TIM crosses to the telephone and starts to dial a number. DAVID looks up and gathers his strength.

DAVID:　　What … are you doing?

TIM:　　　You need a doctor. I'm phoning the hospital …

DAVID:　　No, wait! Wait a minute! Tim, please!

TIM looks across at DAVID; hesitates, then replaces the phone. He crosses to DAVID.

DAVID:　　(*Speaking with an effort*) Are you going to give Colby the card?

TIM:　　　(*Quietly*) Yes, David.

DAVID:　　It's got my name on it …

TIM:　　　(*Looking at the card*) It hasn't got any names on it, I told you …

DAVID:　　(*In great pain*) Yes … Yes, it has, Tim. When it's processed there's my name and … and …

TIM kneels down by the chair.

TIM:　　　David, what is this? What's it all about?

DAVID speaks with an effort; he holds TIM's arm for support.

DAVID: There's – there's been a group of us …
            We've been smuggling diamonds …
TIM: The Arlington Ring?
DAVID: Yes.
TIM: Are you one of the Arlington Ring?
DAVID: Yes … Lewis found out about us, but he
            didn't know I was a member. He promised to
            send Fenby the details – then one night … the
            night he was killed … he discovered that I …
            I …

DAVID falls forward from the chair.
TIM: David!
*The shot becomes blurred and begins to shimmer as if we are
seeing DAVID's features reflected in a pool of water.*

DISSOLVE TO: *A shot of the postcard in a deep tray of
liquid; the card is being processed. Over the drawing of the
girl's hand and the Chianti bottle appear the words: "Dear
Peter …" Before the rest of the message appears:*

CUT TO: A Laboratory at Scotland Yard.
*DETECTIVE INSPECTOR LAYTON and MORGAN, a white-
coated (Police) Laboratory Assistant are standing beside the
tray.*
LAYTON: Is it coming through all right?
MORGAN: Yes. (*Amused; pointing to the tray*) This
            wasn't necessary you know …
LAYTON: What do you mean?
MORGAN: Anyone could have read the card with an
            ultra-violet light.
LAYTON: (*Nodding*) Yes; a certain Mr Fenby did.
            Make copies and let me have them in an hour.
MORGAN: Yes, sir.

CUT TO: COLBY's Office.

COLBY is at the desk writing a report. LAYTON enters carrying a folder; he puts the folder down on the desk.

LAYTON: Copies of the card, sir.

COLBY: Thank you. (*He finishes the report and puts down his pen*) Is Tim Forester here?

LAYTON: Yes; he's just returned from the hospital.

COLBY: Is there any news about his brother?

LAYTON: (*Nodding*) He'll pull through all right; but he refuses to make a statement.

COLBY: All right – send Forester in. I'd like to see him.

LAYTON: Right …

LAYTON goes out. COLBY opens the folder and takes out the postcard. He is looking at this when LAYTON returns with TIM who looks tired and depressed.

COLBY: Good morning! (*Indicating the chair*) Won't you sit down?

TIM: Thank you.

TIM looks tired and depressed.

COLBY: Mr Forester, we've now had an opportunity of examining the card.

TIM: (*Wearily*) Was it the one you wanted?

COLBY: Yes, it was – and we're very grateful to you for your co-operation.

TIM: (*With almost a sigh*) You said that to me once before, Major Colby.

COLBY: Did I?

TIM: Yes, a long time ago.

COLBY: Forester, I'm awfully sorry about your brother, David. If you could persuade him to make a statement.

TIM: It's no use, I've tried. Did you know – at the very beginning – that he was mixed up in this business?

159

LAYTON: No, we didn't; we began to suspect it after he'd seen Dorking but …

TIM: But you sent him to see Dorking?

LAYTON: Yes, we did.

COLBY: Look, Forester, we need your help. In view of that, I think there are certain things you ought to know.

COLBY looks at the card he is holding, then up at Tim again.

COLBY: Some little time ago your brother, Lewis Forester, read an article by an Italian journalist called Greneko. The article was about an international diamond smuggling organisation known as the Arlington Ring.

TIM: Yes, you told me about that.

LAYTON: Greneko expressed the opinion that the leader of the Ring was British and that the principal members were in fact based in this country.

COLBY: We didn't agree with Greneko; neither did Interpol or the F.B.I. We felt convinced that the Ring had its headquarters in Italy and was predominantly Italian.

LAYTON: Your brother told us that he'd seen Greneko and after making careful investigation he was convinced that the Italian was right. We – er …

LAYTON looks across at COLBY.

COLBY: We advised your brother to stick to his newspaper work and mind his own business. Fortunately, for us, he didn't.

TIM: What do you mean?

COLBY: He continued to make investigations and discovered that the Ring was controlled by someone in this country. He wrote the information, in special ink, on this card and sent it to Fenby.

LAYTON: It was agreed that Fenby should write the story up for the Gazette. Unfortunately, your brother was killed and Fenby has other ideas.

TIM: You mean, he decided to blackmail the Ring.

COLBY: Exactly!

LAYTON: But Fenby wasn't a professional blackmailer, and he didn't quite know how to go about it; so, he got in touch with Reg Dorking. He told Dorking that the card was valuable, but he didn't tell him what was on it. He also, to be on the safe side, supplied him with a dummy card. Dorking was told by Fenby to contact David Forester; he made a mistake and contacted you.

TIM: I see. But Dorking very quickly realised I wasn't the right person because ...

COLBY: Because you didn't use the word Nightingale. He'd been tipped off by Fenby that every legitimate member of the group used the word Nightingale to establish contact.

TIM: How did Fenby know that?

COLBY: (*Holding the card*) It's on the card.

TIM: Is that why Briggs used the word the day he came with the photographs?

LAYTON: Yes; he probably knew that Lewis had a brother that was a member of the Ring, but he wasn't sure whether it was Tim or David.

TIM: But you sent David to see Dorking – why did you do that?

COLBY: Because we thought that Dorking had the card: we took possession of it as soon as David left the hut; but it wasn't the right one.

TIM: (*Thoughtfully*) Someone telephoned David the night I dined with him at St Albans; he mentioned the name Nightingale because I ...

LAYTON: It was Fenby; he wanted David to know that he'd got the card. It was after that that Dorking was told to contact him.

TIM: Only he made a mistake and contacted me.

LAYTON nods.

TIM: How do you know all this about Dorking?

COLBY: Dorking realised that he was on pretty dangerous ground, so he wrote me a letter and deposited it with his bank manager. He then told Fenby that if anything happened to him the letter would be delivered. Fenby lost his temper and beat him up, and when he realised what he'd done he made a dash for it.

TIM: And sent me the card.

COLBY: Yes.

TIM: Why?

COLBY: Well, he says that by that time he realised he was out of his depth and was getting frightened. I think he also realised he'd played your brother Lewis a pretty rotten trick. That's why he sent you the card, instead of me or Layton.

TIM: Because David's name was on it?

COLBY: Yes; if I remember rightly he said – "It's your responsibility from now on".

TIM: Yes. (*Rises; thoughtfully*) I gather you've picked up Fenby.

COLBY: We picked him up last night.

LAYTON: (*Smiling*) Literally …

TIM: What do you mean?

LAYTON: His plane came down in the channel.

COLBY hesitates, then offers TIM the card he is holding.

COLBY: I want you to take a look at this; it's a copy of the card, after it was processed.

TIM takes the card and looks at it.

TIM: (*Astonished; looking up from the card at COLBY*)
            But this name, the second one, surely …
COLBY: (*Nodding*) That's the person we're really after, Mr
            Forester. That's why we need your help.
TIM looks again at the card. He is still bewildered.

CUT TO: *ALISON is walking down a country lane towards
a telephone box: she carries a telegram in her hand. She
enters the box.*

CUT TO: Inside the telephone box.
ALISON lifts the receiver, inserts coins, and dials.

CUT TO: *The telephone on the table in TIM's studio. It is
ringing. TIM lifts the receiver. For the duration of this
conversation, we cut back and forth between TIM and
ALISON.*
TIM: (*On the telephone*) Hello?
ALISON: (*On the other end*) Is that Tim Forester?
TIM: Speaking …
ALISON: This is Alison …
TIM: Oh, hello, Alison!
ALISON: I've just got your telegram.
TIM: Yes, I want to see you, Alison – it's very
            important.
ALISON: What is it – what's happened?
TIM: I'll tell you when I see you. Can you come up to
            Town this afternoon?
ALISON: Yes, if it's necessary.
TIM: I'm afraid it is, Alison – there's something I want
            you to do for me.
ALISON: (*Suspiciously*) Has this got anything to do with my
            father?

TIM: I'll tell you when I see you. Can you be here by two o'clock?

ALISON: (*Puzzled*) Yes, all right.

ALISON replaces the receiver and slowly turns to leave the phone box.

CUT TO: A Bedroom in the Belvedere Hotel, Bloomsbury.

NORMAN BRIGGS is packing his suitcase: socks, shirts, ties, etc are on the bed. BRIGGS is taking his time over the packing. A portable radio is playing music. After a little while there is a knock on the door.

BRIGGS: (*Not looking up*) Come in!

The door is heard opening and closing.

BRIGGS: (*Still at the suitcase*) It's nearly twenty minutes since I rang. Bring me a pot of tea and some buttered toast.

BRIGGS turns and stops dead; dropping the socks he is holding, into the case.

BRIGGS: (*Astonished*) Why, Alison!

Alison is standing by the door, looking at BRIGGS. She looks tense and a shade nervous.

ALISON: (*Quietly*) Hello, Father …

BRIGGS: Alison, I didn't expect you, I thought …

ALISON: (*Indicating the suitcase*) Are you going away again?

BRIGGS moves towards ALISON.

BRIGGS: Yes, I'm leaving tomorrow morning, I …

BRIGGS switches off the radio.

BRIGGS: Alison, why haven't you been in touch with me? Why did you leave Sorrento like that?

ALISON: (*Tensely*) You know why, Father …

BRIGGS: (*Shaking his head*) No, I don't. I don't know why. I thought you were killed in that car crash. It wasn't until I got to England that I suspected …

164

ALISON: That you suspected – what?

BRIGGS: Alison, why have you done this to me? All I asked you to do was to find out a few details about a complete stranger – a man you'd never even seen before.

ALISON: Instead of which, I found out a few details about you, Father.

BRIGGS: What do you mean?

ALISON: I know what you've been doing. I know all about the Arlington Ring, I …

BRIGGS: (*Quickly; tensely*) Who told you that? Who told you about the Ring?

ALISON: Lewis Forester told me, he said – that's why he followed you to Sorrento.

BRIGGS: (*Facing ALISON*) Forester sent a card to a friend of his – it had details of the Arlington Ring on it, including certain names. My name's on the card, isn't it, Alison?

ALISON: I don't know, I know nothing about the card. (*Tensely*) Father, there's something I've got to ask you – something I've got to know.

BRIGGS: Well?

ALISON: (*Watching BRIGGS*) Did you murder that girl – Jill Stewart?

BRIGGS: (*Shocked*) Why, no! No, of course I didn't! Whatever gave you that idea?

ALISON: She was found in Tim Forester's Studio.

BRIGGS: Well – why should that incriminate me?

ALISON: (*Quietly*) You've got a key to the flat, haven't you?

BRIGGS: (*After a moment*) Yes. The key was left in the door the second time I went there, the time I took the dress. Forester left me alone for a little while: he went out to get the wire-model. While he was out, I made an impression of the key.

ALISON: (*Slowly*) But you didn't murder Jill Stewart?

BRIGGS: No, I didn't, Alison! I swear to you I didn't.

ALISON: Why did you want my portrait painting?

BRIGGS: I didn't. I took the photographs to Tim Forester: one, because I knew either David or Tim was a member of the group and I wanted to find out which one it was – and, two: I thought if you'd already contacted Forester he'd give the game away when he saw the photographs.

ALISON: I see.

BRIGGS: Later, after I'd delivered the dress, I realised I'd made a mistake. Only Lewis Forester knew of my association with the Ring; so far as the police were concerned, I didn't exist. I decided to recover both the dress and the photographs; without them, there was no proof that I'd ever visited Forester.

ALISON: But you returned the dress and the photographs.

BRIGGS: Yes.

ALISON: Why?

BRIGGS: Because when I was in Rome, I read about the murder of Jill Stewart and Tim Forester's statement about the dress. I knew, of course, that he'd made a mistake and that the dress was a different one, but I also knew that if the police believed his story, they'd be on the look-out for me. In fact, they'd think it was suspicious if I didn't put in an appearance. I decided my best bet was to return the dress and pretend to be mystified by the whole business.

ALISON: I see.

A pause. ALISON looks at her father; it is difficult to tell what she is thinking.

BRIGGS: Alison, I've done some pretty rotten things in my time, but I swear to you – I didn't murder Jill Stewart.

ALISON: Then who did?

BRIGGS: I – don't know.

ALISON: (*Shaking her head; tensely*) I don't believe you!

BRIGGS: Alison, I swear …

ALISON: (*Facing him; angry*) I don't believe you!

BRIGGS: (*A moment; turning away*) All right, if you don't believe me, there's nothing more to be said.

ALISON: There's a great deal more to be said and if you've got any sense, you'll say it!

BRIGGS: What do you mean?

ALISON: Go straight to the police and tell them the whole story, tell them …

BRIGGS: (*Astonished*) So that's why you came here! Do you think I'm crazy? For years I've been in this game and they haven't got a thing on me! If I go to the police now …

ALISON: They've got the card, there's enough information on that to …

BRIGGS: (*Angry; more sure of himself*) Listen, I don't give two hoots in hell about the card!

ALISON: Then why are you running away?

BRIGGS: (*A moment, then:*) Because I'm retiring, Alison. I'm walking out.

ALISON: Is it so easy to walk out on people like that?

BRIGGS: What do you mean?

ALISON: You must know a great deal about them, do you think they'll let you walk out on them, just – just like that?

BRIGGS: I'm no fool. I know when to talk and when to keep my mouth shut. This is the time to keep it shut.

ALISON: (*Quietly*) All right, Father …

ALISON turns towards the door.

BRIGGS: Alison …

ALISON turns.

ALISON: Yes?

BRIGGS: I may not see you again, at least – not for a very long time. Is there anything you want?

ALISON: (*Shaking her head; bitterly*) No; no, nothing.

BRIGGS: If it's a question of money …

ALISON: It isn't a question of anything!

ALISON moves towards the door, then stops. After a moment, she turns, and looks at BRIGGS again.

ALISON: Yes, there is one thing …

BRIGGS: Well?

ALISON: I want you to give me something.

BRIGGS: Yes, Alison, of course – what is it?

ALISON: (*Facing Briggs; a moment, then:*) I want the key.

BRIGGS: (*Puzzled*) The key? Which key?

ALISON: The key to Tim Forester's flat.

BRIGGS: (*Without thinking*) I'm afraid I haven't got it. I gave it to … (*He stops*)

ALISON: You gave it to the man who murdered Jill Stewart!

BRIGGS: (*Tensely; shaking his head; trying to convince ALISON*) Yes, but I didn't know that was going to happen. I never thought, not for one moment, that … Alison, you've got to believe me!

ALISON stands looking at BRIGGS.

CUT TO: The Hospital Bed – as in Episode 5.

REG DORKING is standing by the bed, dressing himself. His head and face are still heavily bandaged, and it is obviously a very great effort for him to get dressed. He is struggling with his jacket when an elderly SISTER appears.

SISTER: (*Astonished*) Mr Dorking! What on earth do you think you're doing?

DORKING: Well, I'm not doing a striptease!

SISTER: The doctor distinctly said that you were not to leave the hospital until Tuesday.

DORKING: The doctor's nuts! I'm leaving!

DORKING picks up his wallet and watch from the table. He takes a card from the wallet.

DORKING: Do you run a car?

SISTER: (*Puzzled*) Why, no.

DORKING: (*Handing SISTER the card*) You should. Look me up sometime.

DORKING leaves. The SISTER looks at the card she is holding.

CUT TO: A Bedroom in the Belvedere Hotel, Bloomsbury.

NORMAN BRIGGS is in the hotel bedroom, still packing and sorting out various odds and ends. He puts a handkerchief in the suitcase. The radio is playing. The telephone rings and BRIGGS turns from the suitcase, turns down the radio, and lifts the telephone receiver.

BRIGGS: (*On the phone*) Hello?

GIRL: (*On the other end*) Mr Briggs?

BRIGGS: Yes.

GIRL: This is the Reception Desk, sir – there's a gentleman to see you.

BRIGGS: (*Surprised*) To see me? I'm not expecting anyone.

GIRL: It's a Mr Nightingale, sir.

169

BRIGGS: (*After a moment; serious*) All right. Send him up.
BRIGGS slowly replaces the receiver. He looks thoughtful.

CUT TO: TIM's Studio Flat.
TIM, ALISON, COLBY and LAYTON are present. ALISON sitting on the wing chair; TIM on the arm of the chair, LAYTON near an easel and COLBY by the dais, looking towards ALISON.

COLBY: In other words, you don't really think your visit made any difference, Miss Ford.

ALISON: No, I don't.

LAYTON: You don't think he'll change his mind at the last minute?

ALISON: He won't change his mind, Inspector – I'm sure of it.

COLBY moves towards ALISON.

TIM: (*Rising, to LAYTON*) Look, Inspector, you know Briggs is one of the Ring – his name's on the card – so why don't you just pick him up?

LAYTON: The fact that his name's on the card is proof so far as we're concerned, because we know that your brother Lewis knew what he was talking about. But it's not evidence, it wouldn't amount to that –

LAYTON snaps his fingers.

LAYTON: – in a court of Law.

COLBY: (*Seriously; a shade tense*) We've got to make either your brother or Briggs talk. Now if we do that …

TIM: (*Shaking his head*) David won't talk – he won't even see me …

COLBY: Then it's got to be Briggs!

ALISON: But my father's leaving the country tomorrow.

LAYTON: Yes, we know, Miss Ford. He's booked on the ten o'clock plane to Montreal.

COLBY: (*To LAYTON; with authority*) Let him get through the Customs and the currency people; let him get as far as the plane – let him really think he's getting away with it – then pick him up!

LAYTON: (*Nodding*) Right …

TIM looks across at ALISON who is looking worried and faintly distressed. TIM puts his hand on her shoulder.

CUT TO: *A bedroom door in a corridor at the Belvedere Hotel, Bloomsbury. The number 81 is on the door. A CHAMBERMAID arrives carrying a cup of tea. She takes a pass key – which hangs on a chain from her waist – and opens the door.*

CUT TO: A Bedroom in the Belvedere Hotel, Bloomsbury.

NORMAN BRIGGS is sitting in a chair, fully dressed, facing a small table. His right hand holds an empty glass and dangles over the chair. There is a tray bearing a bottle of whisky and several glasses on the table. BRIGGs looks as if he might be asleep. The door opens and the CHAMBERMAID enters, carrying the cup of tea.

MAID: (*Closing the door behind her*) Good morning, Mr Briggs!

The MAID turns and sees BRIGGS in the chair.

MAID: My word, you're up nice and early this morning!

The MAID crosses to the chair; then stops dead; staring down at BRIGGS. The cup of tea slowly falls from her hand.

CUT TO: COLBY's Office.

MAJOR COLBY is sitting behind his desk, listening to MORGAN. MORGAN still wears his white coat and holds a tumbler containing liquid.

171

MORGAN: … The whole point is, of course, you don't
             need much of this stuff; that's the beauty of it.
             I must confess if I wanted to poison anything
             this is what I'd go for.
COLBY: (*Drily*) I'll bear that in mind, Morgan.
MORGAN: You see, the great thing is there's hardly any
             taste with it, especially in alcohol. I remember
             in nineteen-thirty-nine …
COLBY: (*Rising*) How long does it take before it acts?
MORGAN: Ah, well – it depends on a number of things.
             The heart; the cardiac centre; the central
             nervous system. I remember in nineteen-
             thirty-nine …
COLBY: (*Bluntly*) How long?
MORGAN: It might be fifteen minutes; perhaps even less.
LAYTON enters; he is wearing his overcoat and looks tired.
COLBY: (*To LAYTON; the moment he sees him*) Well
             – did you find her?
LAYTON: (*Wearily*) Yes, I found her. Why do these
             hotel people always live in such God-forsaken
             out of the way places?
COLBY: What did she say?
LAYTON: She confirms what the Manager told us. A
             man turned up at about half-past three, he said
             his name was Nightingale and he asked to see
             Briggs.
COLBY: Did she give you a description?
LAYTON: Yes, but it might have been you or me or
             Morgan or anyone else!
COLBY: What do you mean?
LAYTON: Apparently, he was swathed in bandages –
             one side of his face was completely covered.

COLBY: (*Thoughtfully*) I see. (*Suddenly; making a definite decision*) Phone the Press boys and tell them to go ahead – then contact Forester.

LAYTON: (*Hesitantly*) You think it's a wise move, sir?

COLBY: (*Returning to his desk*) It's our only move, Inspector.

CUT TO: The Front Door of TIM's Flat.
HENRY CARMICHAEL arrives and presses the bell push. He is wearing an overcoat and hat and gloves and carries an evening newspaper. The door is opened by TIM.

TIM: Hello, Carmichael! Come in!
HENRY enters.

CUT TO: The Entrance Hall of TIM's Flat.

HENRY: Am I too early for you?

TIM: No, you said six o'clock. Let me take your hat and coat.

HENRY: Oh, thank you.
HENRY takes off his overcoat.

CUT TO: TIM's Studio Flat.
TIM enters followed by CARMICHAEL.

TIM: Can I offer you a drink?

HENRY: Oh – er – have you a ginger ale?

TIM: Yes, of course. Is that all you want – a ginger ale, Henry?

HENRY: Well, I'll join you. Two fingers please.
TIM crosses to the drinks cabinet and mixes two drinks.

HENRY: Were you surprised when I phoned you?

TIM: (*At the cabinet*) Yes, I was. Quite frankly, I couldn't understand what you were talking about – that's why I asked you to call round.

173

HENRY: (*Holding out the newspaper*) I was talking about this. Haven't you seen it?

TIM turns, walks over to HENRY with the drinks. HENRY takes a glass from TIM and TIM takes the newspaper which he looks at. We see the Stop Press Column of the newspaper. An announcement reads: Police report new development in Jill Stewart murder; arrest believed to be imminent.

TIM: (*Looking up at HENRY*) No, this is news to me.

HENRY: (*A shade tense*) Tell me – who is it?

TIM: (*Puzzled*) What do you mean – who is it?

HENRY: (*Pointing to the newspaper*) Who is it – who are they going to arrest?

TIM: I don't know; except that I know it's not me.

Tim drinks.

HENRY: (*Quietly*) How do you know it's not you, Forester?

TIM: Well, I – just know, that's all.

HENRY: Have you seen the Inspector lately?

TIM: Yes, he was here yesterday morning.

HENRY: Why?

TIM: It was just a routine call – (*Thoughtfully*) at least, that's what he said.

HENRY looks at TIM and thoughtfully sips his drink; after a moment he puts his drink down on the table.

HENRY: (*Nodding; turning towards the dress on the model*) I see you're still working on the portrait?

TIM: (*Quietly*) Carmichael …

HENRY: Yes?

TIM: (*Pleasantly*) There's something I want to ask you; I meant to ask you the other day.

HENRY: Well?

TIM: You remember the morning you came here – (*Pointing to the dress*) – after the dress had been returned.

HENRY: Yes.

174

TIM: You looked at the dress and said – Isn't this the dress that Jill wore? I said, no – and you said, – well, it looks remarkably like it.

HENRY: Well?

TIM: (*Pleasantly*) How did you know it looks remarkably like it? Had you seen Jill's dress?

HENRY: No, of course I hadn't! She only bought it just before she was murdered …

TIM: (*Still quite pleasant*) And there's another point, Carmichael – it's not really important but I might as well mention it.

HENRY: Yes, indeed. Go on …

TIM: When you wanted to telephone the other day I said – use the extension, it's in the bedroom.

HENRY: Well?

TIM: (*A suggestion of a smile*) I noticed you went straight to the bedroom.

HENRY: Well, what did you expect me to do – jump out of the window? Good heavens, a man with one eye could see that was the bedroom! Look, Forester, are you trying to make out a case against me?

TIM: (*Patting his pockets for his cigarette case*) Now don't be silly, old boy – why should I want to do that?

HENRY assures Tim; he isn't at all sure of him.

TIM: You don't happen to have a cigarette on you?

HENRY: (*Faintly irritated and annoyed*) I'm afraid I don't.

TIM turns and crosses to the drinks cabinet; he opens the cabinet and searches for a packet of cigarettes. HENRY picks up his drink and stands watching TIM; he doesn't look at all happy. Suddenly he looks down at the glass in his hand, then across at TIM. He hesitates, then takes a tablet out of his waistcoat pocket and drops it into his own glass; he stirs the liquid with his finger, dissolving the tablet. TIM returns to Henry, opening a packet of cigarettes.

TIM: Would you like a cigarette?

HENRY: (*Watching TIM*) Thank you.

HENRY puts his glass down on the table next to TIM's. Approximately the same amount of liquid is in each and the shape and the size of the glasses is the same. HENRY accepts a cigarette from Tim and offers him a light.

HENRY: Have you any other interesting questions, Mr Forester?

TIM: (*Pleasantly*) Yes, as a matter of fact I have.

TIM picks up the newspaper and indicates the stop press column.

TIM: Is this the only reason you wanted to see me?

HENRY: Yes. If the police really have found out who murdered Jill ...

TIM: You'd like to know who it is.

HENRY: Naturally.

TIM: Well, why don't you ring the Inspector?

HENRY: I can't very well do that.

TIM: (*Holding out the newspaper*) Did you think this referred to me?

HENRY: (*After a moment's hesitation*) I wondered. (*Suddenly*) Don't misunderstand me, Forester. I don't think you did murder Jill, otherwise I wouldn't be here, but I wondered if ...

TIM: If I was still under suspicion?

HENRY: Yes.

TIM: Well, I'm not.

HENRY looks at TIM for a moment, and then picks up a glass off the table.

HENRY: You know, you must have been in a pretty tight spot at one time.

TIM: I was. (*Smiling*) But thanks to you I got out of it.

176

HENRY: Why, thanks to me?

TIM: You told me about Alison Ford. You told me what a bad character she was, and how she threatened to murder Jill.

HENRY: Yes, but Alison's dead.

TIM: (*Shaking his head*) Alison's not dead; she's alive, very much alive.

HENRY: Good God! (*Pointing to the newspaper in TIM's hand*) You mean – they suspected Alison?

TIM: (*Putting down the newspaper and picking up the remaining drink from the table*) No, that's not what I mean. When you told me about Alison, I knew perfectly well that you'd seen Briggs and that he'd asked you to corroborate the story he'd already told me about Alison.

HENRY: Briggs? Who the devil is Briggs?

TIM: You know who Briggs is – the man you saw yesterday afternoon at the Belvedere Hotel.

HENRY: The man I saw yesterday after … Look, have you gone crazy, Forester? I've never heard of Briggs! I wouldn't know him if he walked into this room!

TIM: Wouldn't you?

TIM turns, crosses and goes into the dressing-room. HENRY looks towards the dressing-room, obviously puzzled. He finishes his drink and puts the empty glass down on the table. TIM returns carrying a photograph.

TIM: For your information, that's Mr Briggs.

HENRY takes the photograph and looks at it. It is a photograph of BRIGGS. HENRY hands the photograph back to Tim.

HENRY: I've never seen this man before!

TIM: You're lying, Carmichael!

HENRY: I tell you I'm not lying! I've never seen him before!

Tim puts down the photograph and takes a drink out of his glass and looks across at HENRY.

TIM: (*Slowly; quietly*) Carmichael, shall I prove to you that you're lying? Shall I prove that …

TIM stops and looks at the glass he is holding.

TIM: (*Casually*) Oh, I'm sorry, I've taken your drink.

HENRY: (*Softly; stunned*) What?

TIM: (*Putting his glass down*) It's nothing: I must have picked up your drink by mistake, that's all. Carmichael, shall I prove to you that …

HENRY: (*Suddenly; taking hold of TIM's arm*) What do you mean – picked up my drink by mistake?

TIM: (*With a shrug*) It's not important.

HENRY: (*Quickly; tensely*) It is important! It's damned important! What do you mean?

TIM: (*Smiling*) Well, either I picked your drink up, or you picked mine up; in either case it's not important …

HENRY: (*Holding TIM's arm*) How do you know?

TIM: (*Pleasantly*) How do I know what?

HENRY: (*Pointing to the glass in TIM's hand*) How do you know that's my drink?

TIM: (*Releasing his arm; pointing to HENRY's glass*) That glass is chipped; I purposely didn't give it to you.

HENRY: (*Staggered; moving back from TIM*) My God! (*Moves towards the alcove*) I've got to go, Forester, I'm in a hurry, I …

TIM: (*Holding HENRY's arm*) Oh, no – not yet, Carmichael. We haven't finished our little chat.

HENRY: (*Alarmed*) Listen, Forester, you don't understand …

TIM: I understand perfectly.

HENRY: No, no, you don't. I've taken poison; I've got to see a doctor; I've got …

TIM takes hold of HENRY and pushes him towards the wing chair.

TIM: Sit down, Carmichael!

HENRY: (*Struggling to free himself*) Forester, don't be a fool! Don't you understand, I've taken poison! I've got to get out of here; I've got to get out of here; I've got to have an antidote.

TIM: (*Quite tough; forcing HENRY into the chair*) I'm the antidote! I'm just what the doctor ordered!

TIM pulls up the table, and sits on the edge of it, facing HENRY, almost pinning him in the chair.

HENRY: Forester, let me go! Don't you understand, if I don't get to a hospital I'll die!

TIM: And, of course, <u>you</u> mustn't die, must you, Carmichael?

HENRY: (*Softly*) What do you mean?

TIM: (*Leaning towards HENRY; quietly*) You murdered Jill Stewart, didn't you?

HENRY: (*A shade frightened*) No …

TIM: You murdered Jill, didn't you, Carmichael?

HENRY: No! No, I didn't. I swear to you I … (*Desperate, trying to get out of the chair*) Look, I've got to get out of here, I've got to …

TIM rises and hits CARMICHAEL on the shoulder; he falls back into the chair.

TIM: (*Relentlessly*) You murdered Jill, didn't you?

HENRY looks at TIM; he is frightened, getting desperate.

HENRY: Yes …

TIM: Why?

HENRY: She was playing fast and loose with me … the little devil kept leading me on … I never knew

179

from one day to the next whether she intended to marry me or not.

TIM: That wasn't your only reason, was it, Carmichael?

HENRY: (*A moment*) No, she knew I was mixed up in something and started to make inquiries. Sooner or later, she'd have found out about the Arlington Ring. (*Tensely; taking hold of TIM's arm*) Forester, I've got to get to a hospital, there isn't much time.

TIM: (*Pushing HENRY's arm away; forcing him back into the chair*) What happened that night – the night I was in St Albans?

HENRY: (*Tensely*) Briggs told me he had a key to your flat, I took the key – came here – telephoned Jill. I said it was you – I said you'd changed your mind about dining with your brother and you wanted to see her. She – came – here – she was wearing the dress, the one she'd bought in South Audley Street.

TIM: Go on …

HENRY: We had a row and I – lost my temper.

TIM: (*Tense; leaning forward*) What about the Chianti? Why did Jill ask me to deliver a bottle of Chianti to you?

HENRY: She didn't.

TIM: (*Surprised*) She didn't?

HENRY: No, I brought the bottle here …

TIM: (*Astonished*) You did?

HENRY: Yes.

TIM: When?

HENRY: The same night; the night I met Jill. Briggs had given it to me. I had to send it to one of our agents in Ireland – a man called Walters. Walters was supposed to take it with him to New York. It was a means of identification.

TIM suddenly rises and points to the bedroom.

TIM: My God, I've got it! You strangled Jill – rushed out of the bedroom – and picked up the wrong parcel! You picked up the parcel that Jill gave me.

HENRY: (*Moving out of the chair; looking towards the alcove*) Yes …

TIM: What was in that parcel?

HENRY: Just a pair of slippers …

TIM: (*Softly; to himself*) Well, I'm damned!

HENRY suddenly rushes across the room and out through the alcove. TIM makes no attempt to stop him. Slowly, thoughtfully, TIM turns towards the dressing-room. MAJOR COLBY comes out of the dressing-room, carrying a glass; it is the glass into which HENRY dropped the tablet – TIM having exchanged the glasses when he went into the dressing-room for the photograph of BRIGGS.

COLBY: (*Pleasantly*) Thank you, Mr Forester.

TIM: (*Quietly; indicating the drink*) Did he poison it?

COLBY: You'd have very soon found out if you'd drunk it.

In the background, from somewhere in the building, there is the noise of a brawl and HENRY's voice raised in anger. LAYTON enters from the alcove.

COLBY: (*To LAYTON*) Everything all right, Inspector?

LAYTON: Yes, we've just picked him up.

COLBY: (*With a gesture*) What about the boys upstairs?

LAYTON: They're very happy; it was a perfect recording.

COLBY: (*To TIM*) You certainly went to Town on him; I didn't know you were that tough!

TIM: (*Rather pleased with himself*) I'll have you know when I was at Oxford, I was the welter-weight champion.

181

LAYTON: (*With a twinkle in his eye*) Indeed, sir? I'm glad you didn't tell us before.

COLBY: (*Smiling and shaking his head sadly*) If we'd known that we should have been much nicer to you, Mr Forester.

CUT TO: TIM's Studio flat. Several weeks later.

TIM is working on the portrait of ALISON. The doorbell rings, and TIM puts down his brush and palette and goes across to the alcove.

CUT TO: The Entrance Hall of TIM's Flat.

TIM opens the front door. ALISON is in the doorway.

TIM: (*Surprised and delighted*) Alison!

ALISON: (*Smiling*) Hello, Tim!

TIM: Where on earth have you been? I sent three telegrams; I went down to Box Hill, I … Come in!

CUT TO: TIM's Studio Flat.

ALISON enters followed by TIM.

TIM: Let me take your coat!

ALISON: No, I can't stay very long, Tim. I've got to …

TIM: (*Taking ALISON's coat*) Nonsense!

TIM puts the coat down on the arm of the wing chair.

TIM: (*Facing ALISON*) Look, Alison, what happened? I wrote you letters, I sent you telegrams, I …

ALISON: Yes, I'm awfully sorry, Tim. I ought to have telephoned you or something, but –

ALISON turns away from TIM; near to tears.

ALISON: I've been away.

TIM: (*Gently*) Where have you been?

ALISON: Oh, just – away.

ALISON turns towards TIM again.

TIM: Well, you look jolly well, Alison. Do you feel better?

ALISON: (*Nodding; forcing a smile*) Yes, I do.

TIM: (*Smiling*) Well, in that case, I forgive you for not writing, or phoning, or calling, or telegraming.

ALISON: Now you're really making me feel a beast!

TIM: Good! Let me get you some tea.

ALISON: (*Stopping him*) No, I can't stay, Tim! I've got an awful lot of packing to do and …

TIM: (*Seriously*) What do you mean – packing?

ALISON: I'm leaving for Paris tonight; I'm going to stay with some friends for two or three months.

TIM: (*After a moment; looking at ALISON*) Do you think that's a good idea?

ALISON: Yes, I do.

TIM: Well, I don't. I think it's a rotten idea!

ALISON: Why?

TIM: Because you don't want to go to Paris – you don't want to stay with friends – you're just running away.

ALISON: That's not true!

TIM: You know it is, Alison.

ALISON: No, Tim. (*Shaking her head; a shade emotional*) No; I'd stay only – there's just nothing for me to stay for.

TIM: (*Quietly*) I think there is.

ALISON looks at TIM; there is a pause, then:

ALISON: (*Bright; yet almost on the defence*) What have you been doing during the past two or three weeks?

TIM: Oh – just working on the portrait.

ALISON: How's it going?

ALISON moves across to the dais; followed by TIM.

TIM: Not very well. I don't think working from
            photographs is ever really satisfactory.
ALISON: (*Hesitantly*) Well – why don't you give it up?
TIM: (*Moving nearer to ALISON*) I don't want to.
ALISON: Too much like running away?
TIM: Alison …
ALISON: Yes?
TIM: Why don't you sit for me?
ALISON: (*After a pause; nodding towards the dress on the
            model*) In the dress?
TIM: (*A moment; looking down at ALISON*) No. Not in
            that dress, Alison – just as you are.
ALISON: Wouldn't that mean you'd have to start all over
            again?
TIM: Is that such a bad idea?
ALISON: But – I should be here for quite a while, shouldn't
            I?
TIM: (*Suggestion of a smile*) Quite a while.
ALISON: Days at least.
TIM: Probably weeks.
ALISON: As long as that?
TIM: I once took six months to paint a little brown jug.
ALISON: Am I more difficult than a little brown jug?
TIM: Infinitely. (*Moving nearer to ALISON*) But much
            prettier. (*Suddenly*) Alison, can you make coffee;
            good, strong, black coffee?
ALISON: (*Slightly taken aback*) Yes, I can as a matter of
            fact. Why?
TIM: (*Putting his arm around ALISON's waist*) I
            wondered, that's all.
ALISON: (*Looking up at TIM*) Do you always have coffee
            for breakfast, Mr Forester?

*TIM looks at ALISON, and suddenly starts laughing. He pulls
ALISON towards him.*

THE END

Press Pack

Press cuttings about *Portrait of Alison* …

New Thriller Serial

Actor-of-the year Patrick Barr will be appearing in a new thriller serial next month. It is called *Portrait of Alison*.

"Can't tell you much about it," Barr told me, "because as far as I know I'm the only person cast. I play the painter."

Portrait of Alison is written by Francis Durbridge who wrote *The Teckman Biography*, the outstanding tv thriller of last year.

Patrick Barr's performance in that serial helped to gain him his actor-of-the-year award of course.

Mr Barr, plus Mr Durbridge, adds up to good entertainment.

News Chronicle

Top TV Actor and Thrill Man Team Up

Television's "Actor of the Year" and its foremost thriller writer are collaborating in the new, mid-week serial, *Portrait of Alison* that begins this month.

Patrick Barr – you can see him on Sunday get his award – is the actor. The writer is Francis Durbridge who wrote what was probably television's best yet serial thriller, *The Teckman Biography*. Durbridge's sense of the visual and his craftmanship are outstanding among television writers. He specialises in taut, swift stories.

The success of his *Teckman Biography* was unique in British television. It was subsequently filmed and sired a popular tune.

Evening Chronicle

The name of Francis Durbridge on a television serial is sufficient guarantee of first-class quality. His latest, *Portrait of Alison*, which began last night promises to be as good as, if not better than its forerunners. Mr Durbridge is the master of suspense and he leaves us at a point in the story which compels us to make a date with him the following week.

There is never any padding in the Durbridge thrillers. So many of the tv serials have been spun out with extraneous matter; not so with Mr Durbridge. He makes every line of the script count and red herrings are pulled across our path until we are suspecting almost everybody at the end of half an hour.

We are left at the end of the first episode with a pretty girl murdered and the hero under suspicion. Patrick Barr plays the role of the artist in whose room the crime takes place. This murder somehow links up with the death of his brother in a car crash in Italy. *Portrait of Alison* certainly will keep me from making any engagements for the next five Wednesday evenings.

Northern Despatch

Francis Durbridge's new thriller serial *Portrait of Alison* is the old master of suspense at his best. It's the crispest, most exciting serial since his *Teckman Biography* almost a year ago.

Last night's first episode underlined just how far ahead of his competitors is the adroit Mr Durbridge. It had a sureness of touch that must have made them turn from their typewriters in despair.

Evening Chronicle

The Crooks Are Wonderful Too ...
The rule for Wednesday night serials: – either they start so badly that they must improve, or they start well and slop.

188

Portrait of Alison is the rare example. It started well and it gets better and better. Never have 30 minutes been so crowded.

The smallest parts are impeccably played. Anthony Nicholls has made a real character of Scotland Yard's Major Colby and William Lucas as the shady car dealer is a gem.

To keep up this level of episodic thrill, Francis Durbridge should at once inaugurate a BBC school for TV script writers and teach them the tricks of the trade.

Birmingham Gazette

Let Yourself Be Bamboozled

Someone with more faith in my powers of detection than I have myself, asked me the other day who I considered to be the criminal in the television serial *Portrait of Alison*.

What a question and as if it mattered! I suppose the author, Francis Durbridge, does know before he starts on these stories who is going to be unmasked in the long run, but to those of us who merely watch the thing it seems a most hopeless jumble and I defy anyone to try and work out things to a logical conclusion.

This is one thing you must not do with a story like this. Mr Durbridge did not win his spurs with Paul Temple for nothing. He knows the value of a red herring and those mystifying endings of his. What on earth is going to happen tonight I wonder?

The thing to do is to sit back and enjoy the smooth, highly professional technique of bamboozling and, when the last episode arrives, to look judicial and indicate that this was just how you had worked it out from the beginning. If you play your cards right, you will get away with it. I invariably do.

Evening Sentinel

Red Herrings by **Barrie Heads**

Speaking quite personally, I would not trust Peter Fenby as far as I could throw him. Or Mr Briggs, for that matter. But then I have suspicions about Major Colby. And if it comes to that, there's something very fishy about that chap Dorking – you know, the one who got knocked on the head this week – and about David Forester. Calls himself a schoolmaster, doesn't he? Well, that's his story. One or two others I could name also. Not entirely above board, I should say.

It is a measure of the continued success of the serial *Portrait of Alison* – and to a certain extent a measure of the comparative monotony of the rest of the week – that one becomes somehow involved in its plot and counterplot, anxious for the slipping into gear of the next improbable cog, infuriated that the end leaves one still baffled. Francis Durbridge has written one of the best tv serials yet shown, full of suspense, full of action, reeking deliciously of red herrings.

Yorkshire Post

Mystery Man Francis Is A 9 to 5 Man by **Max North**

"What next?" I asked Francis Durbridge, the author of *Portrait of Alison*, the tv serial success which ends next week.

"What next in what direction?" parried the prolific Mr Durbridge. "Films? Books? Sound radio? Or television?" He forgot to mention, too, his strip cartoon story which runs in the *Manchester Evening News* each night.

"In television," I replied.

"Well, I have signed a contract with the BBC to write two television serials a year for five-years. You probably know that."

I said I did and was glad about it.

"That doesn't start until the end of the year. So there will be a bit of a gap. I am writing another Paul Temple serial for sound radio. I have a book to write. Oh, and they're going to film *Portrait of Alison*."

"About that BBC contract, Mr Durbridge – I am told it is worth about £250 per instalment £8 a minute."

"Oh, well, I'm afraid I can't go into that. I haven't said that. I don't like to talk about that sort of thing."

"But I can say it makes you one of the highest-paid writers of today?"

"Yes, you can say that."

The value of the contract – believed to be the highest ever offered to a writer by the BBC – is the only mystery surrounding Mr Durbridge, master mystery writer.

Mild, softly spoken, 42 years old, he lives with his wife and two sons at Walton-on-Thames, 40 minutes by car from the Lime Grove Studios, where he personally assists his serials into production.

At nine in the morning, he goes into his study. He writes first in longhand and then at a typewriter. "No one else can read my writing," he explains. "Then I send the whole thing to a girl to be retyped."

At five in the afternoon, he reappears. His relaxations are disappointing to followers of his serials: he reads or goes to the theatre. He assures me has never been involved with a Major Colby type from the Special Branch.

Nothing exciting ever seems to happen to Mr Durbridge.

"I'm just a professional writer," he says.

Manchester Evening News

Did the Villain Take <u>You</u> By Surprise?
Six weeks of suspense were ended by the final instalment of *Portrait of Alison* which must rank as one of television's best serials. Francis Durbridge never lets up on the thrills and yet always persuades us that such things can happen. A very professional performance.

It is easy to be wise after the event, and say it was obvious who the real villain was, but to be honest, I had never spotted them. My chief suspect did not even appear in the last instalment.

The suspense could have been even better contained, though, had the BBC been more cautious in billing each week's cast. We were told a week in advance that Alison had never been killed, because she was due to appear in Episode 3. Last night I knew it could not be Peter Fenby after all, because he had faded out over the course of the programme.

Patrick Barr, inevitably, acted brilliantly throughout. Anthony Nicholls as the top-secret sleuth working with Interpol and the FBI has established a character I hope to see in still more adventures. But my own especial fancy of the serial has been William Lucas, whose portrayal of a spiv car salesman was brilliant.

Birmingham Mail

The Tension Is Over

Now we know who killed the model in the Francis Durbridge thriller *Portrait of Alison* and what all the suspicious characters were up to. It has been the best serial on tv to date and unlike some it did not peter out in the last episode. The viewer might have had suspicions but he could not be absolutely sure until halfway through the final programme.

What helped to make it such an outstanding thriller was the fact Mr Durbridge made his solution credible. Often a thriller holds our attention then the climax disappoints because it is so impossible; this was not the case in *Portrait of Alison*.

The individual performances through the six episodes have been excellent with Patrick Barr adding further to his laurels.

Northern Despatch

Midlands-Born Author Hits TV Jackpot

The success story of star serial scribe Francis Durbridge runs into yet another instalment. The Midlands born and bred man who has written thrills for millions in his adventures of the radio detective Paul Temple has hit the jackpot again – on television.

His fourth tv serial, *Portrait of Alison*, is one of his best. It will follow its three predecessors, on to the cinema screen, for film rights have now been bought for a hefty sum.

The Broken Horseshoe, Operation Diplomat, The Teckman Biography – they all made screen fare. *Portrait of Alison* should transfer equally well to celluloid.

The man whose characters have become known in homes all over Great Britain shuns the limelight himself. To information seekers he says: "I don't encourage personal publicity. And I never discuss the financial rewards for my work."

But here is a brief Portrait of Durbridge. At 42, he is baldish, prosperous, tolerant, hard-working, and a non-smoker. He lives in Surrey with his wife and two sons.

His address – the Moat House, Walton-on-Thames – sounds like a country house at which detective Temple might keep a nocturnal rendezvous to hear "something to his advantage." But Durbridge asserts it is a perfectly ordinary building with no sinister connections.

Birmingham is his home town, he went to school near there, and studied at Birmingham University. And it was in the Midlands that his greatest brainchild – detective-novelist Paul Temple – was "born."

Since the first instalment of his first serial involving this suave, sophisticated sleuth went over the air from the BBC's Birmingham studios in April 1938, Mr Temple has thought his way through 11 adventures, netting his creator thousands of pounds.

And the best news for Temple's thousands of fans is that there is another serial tapping out on the Durbridge typewriter. Meanwhile, to keep them happy a repeat of one of the best-known adventures – *The Madison Case* – will probably be heard in the Light Programme in a few months.

Temple has his worshippers in many other parts of the world, Australia, New Zealand, and all over Europe. Excerpts from his casebook have been translated into most European languages. The Danish State Radio broadcast of the *Gregory Affair* last autumn created such interest that even cinemas interrupted their programmes to broadcast the last episode of the story.

Temple has also made a hit on the screen, and become the hero of many a strip cartoon.

As a schoolboy, young Master Durbridge's mind was taken up with detectives. At 15 he wrote a mystery thriller called *The Great Dutton*. It was performed in aid of charity at a Liverpool hostel.

While at university he wrote and played in a revue. In the audience was a Mr Webster, now known to listeners as Martyn C. Webster, producer of the Paul Temple plays. "He thought I was quite the worst actor he had ever seen," confides Durbridge.

But it was not long before Webster was reading the manuscript of a serious play *Promotion* brought to him by the eager youngster who had finished his college career. He produced it in the Midland Region studios, and it met with such success that a sequel entitled *Dolmans* was commissioned.

But the calls of "cops and robbers" still echoed on Durbridge's mind. For some time he had been looking for just the right type of detective to meet his case. And he found him on the train from London to Birmingham.

Durbridge claims that a tall, dark man with a casual ease and friendliness of manner, who sat opposite him on the journey – they did not speak – and got out at Leamington Spa, sparked off a chain of events.

With some professional elaboration, this stranger became the super-sleuth who was to prove the author's biggest radio success.

Switching over to writing for television presented some difficult problems. "I couldn't rely on the same methods I used for sound," says Durbridge. "TV is a very different and difficult medium. You must centre your action on a particular set for some time, to avoid constant switching of the scene. And you can't have a character in a lounge suit one moment and then appearing in evening dress before he has had time to change. Those are only two of the differences."

How does he manage to repeat success after success? Durbridge subscribes to the "ten per cent inspiration, 90 per cent perspiration" idea. He works a normal nine-to-five day in his study at home.

He has no set formula for a successful thriller. "Any thing may set my mind off on a train of thought," he says. "Then I become interested in the characters, and in their particular adventures, and the story develops."

A Durbridge plot is top secret – even from his own family. If they become interested in one of the serials, then they, like all the listeners or viewers, are kept in the dark right until the final episode is transmitted.

Lincolnshire Echo